By Grace I Stand

This is a work of fiction. The characters, incidents, and dialogues are products of the author's imagination. Except for well-known historical and contemporary figures, any resemblance to actual events or persons is entirely coincidental.

Dedication

For my God who loves me unconditionally,
all the time, no matter what.

Yet now he has brought you back as his friends. He has done this through his death on the cross in his own body. As a result he has brought you into the very presence of God, and you are holy and blameless as you stand before him without a single fault.

Colossians 1:22 (NLT)

Chapter One

Dear Amber,

I am so excited we're moving to Sandy! I still can't believe it. I suggested it to my mom and dad on the way home after Grandpa's memorial service, but I never thought they'd actually go for it. I remember praying about it for several days after that, and I kept telling God I would be okay if it didn't happen, but I really wanted it to. And then I stopped praying about it because I knew if it was meant to be, it would happen, and I felt at peace about whatever my parents decided. But when I found out they were actually considering it and my dad was looking for a job up there, I was a complete mess until I heard he actually found one—right in Sandy, no less. Does that sound like God, or what?

I hope you're fine with it. I know you have a lot of other friends, including Seth, and I don't want you to feel like you have to suddenly be my best friend or anything. Just having you there at school will help me with the transition, I'm sure. But I want you to know, Amber, that I really love being around you. I've never met anyone who is so in love with Jesus like you are—and not in a fake way. I hate that worse than someone who doesn't want to know Him at all.

Anyway, we're going to be arriving next Saturday, and my first day at school will be the beginning of the new semester, and if you could help me with finding my classes and stuff, I'd appreciate it. I don't know if I'll see you before then. I think we'll probably go to Grandma's church with her in town, so maybe I'll call you and we can arrange to meet somewhere on the first day.

I also wanted to share with you that my devotions have been really great lately. I think because there's so much going on right now and I've had so much to pray about. It's like I can't wait to have that time, you know? I've never felt that way before. Even when I've been consistent in the past, it's been more because I forced myself to read my Bible than because I really wanted to.

I've also been doing what you suggested about reading one or two verses each day and thinking about how that can apply to my everyday life and asking myself if I'm living that way or not. I've been reading in Colossians because I have been reading through Paul's letters for the past several months. We started in Romans at camp this summer and then when I got finished with that I read Galatians, Ephesians, and Philippians, but I went through them pretty fast and mostly focused on verses I already knew. But I'm not sure I've ever read anything in Colossians before, and so far I've discovered some pretty cool stuff, and I'm still in the first chapter!

My favorite verse so far is verse 13 that says, 'For he has rescued us from the dominion of darkness and brought us into the kingdom of the Son he loves.' Isn't that awesome? I love the mental picture of God reaching down and lifting us out of all the murky confusion, pain, stress, and fear and bringing us into the light where everything is clear and right and beautiful. I want Jesus to sweep through my heart and life and make it shine like only He can.

I will admit I'm a little apprehensive about moving away from here. I do have some friends that I will miss, and six months won't be a lot of time to make a bunch of new ones there, but knowing you'll be there makes me less anxious. I would appreciate your prayers for me. And for my mom. She knows this is what God wants us to do, but she'll be leaving all her friends and my two aunts who live close by. She's been crying a lot, which isn't like her, so I know this is a big deal. I'm glad I didn't try and push anything now because I'd be feeling bad if I thought they were just doing this because I begged them to. I guess I didn't think about my mom having to make all new friends and go to a new church and everything too.

In a million years I never would have thought I'd be excited about moving to a new school halfway through my senior year, but I am, and that's mostly because of you, Amber. I hope you won't be sick of me by February. If you are, please tell me so I won't decide to go to Lifegate with you and drive you nuts for four years!

Love you,
Mandy

"Grace and peace to you from God our Father."
Colossians 1:2

Amber smiled, read through the entire letter again, and then grabbed some stationery from her desk and wrote a letter to Mandy in response.

Okay, it's been six days since I heard the news, and I still can't believe it. I already wrote you a letter on Sunday and sent it to you on Monday, which means you're probably getting it the same day I got yours. But I just wanted to write again and let you know I am thrilled that you're moving here and you better be prepared to be one of my best friends! <u>You'll</u> be sick of <u>me</u> by February! Seriously though, I somehow doubt we'll have any trouble picking up where we left off at Christmas. I've had several really good friends over the years, and every single one of them I knew right away I wanted for a friend. First there was Stacey, who I met in kindergarten, and other than a couple years of us distancing ourselves from one another a bit, we've been great friends ever since. Then there's Nikki, who I met in fifth grade, and we were practically inseparable until one day she accused me of telling a personal secret to a bunch of other people, which I promise I never did, but she stopped speaking to me after that for three years until one day last year when she suddenly trusted me enough to tell me something that was really bothering her, and so now we're friends again and I've sort of become a spiritual mentor to her now, which makes our friendship different than it used to be, but I'm happy to let God use me in her life that way.

And then my sophomore year I met Colleen and she's been a really great friend. I lean on her and she leans on me, and we have a good time together no matter what we're doing. You'll really like her too, and I hope the three of us can be good friends with each other during these last few months of our senior year. Colleen and I were thinking of being college roommates, but it looks like her boyfriend is going to keep going to school in Portland (he's a college freshman this year), and Colleen is thinking she wants to go to the same school he does, which I completely understand since I want to do the same thing.

And then there's Seth. In a million years I never would have imagined he would end up being the best friend I've ever had when I first met him and made a complete idiot of myself, but somehow our hearts connected very quickly and easily, and just when I think we couldn't possibly get any closer, we do.

So anyway, all that to say I know we're going to get along great, Mandy, and I'm sure we'll be there when you arrive to help you get moved in, and I'll definitely show you around on the first day of school. I'll even come by and pick you up a little early so we have plenty of time, and I'll introduce you to all my friends and say, 'If you want to be my friend, you've gotta be hers too!'

See you soon,
Amber

Amber folded the letter, put it in an envelope, and wrote Mandy's name and address on the front. Seeing that her room was a mess, she decided to clean it up a little before dinner. By the time she had everything picked up off the floor, her laundry basket was overflowing and she took it downstairs to put in a load and then stepped into the kitchen just in time to help her mom with setting the table.

"What did Mandy have to say in her letter?" her mom asked.

"She's very excited."

"Told you so."

"She said her mom's having kind of a rough time. They know this is where God wants them, but I suppose suddenly packing up and moving like that would be completely turning your life upside-down."

"I can imagine," her mom agreed. "Aunt Beth is like Mandy. Very sweet but quiet and reserved. But I think I'm almost as excited as you are. Beth probably doesn't think I'll be all that interested in being her friend, but I am. My big sister has always been that: older and bossy. But Beth's not like that at all, and I always enjoy talking with her whenever they visit, so I imagine it will be the same once they're living here."

Amber didn't voice her thoughts, but something occurred to her as she set the glasses on the table and went to get silverware from the drawer: Her mom didn't have a lot of close friendships. She had her older sister, who lived thirty minutes away, and all the women at church liked her mom, and she talked with many of them every Sunday and participated in various ministries and activities with them, but she didn't have anyone she talked to on the phone a lot or went shopping with. Since Stacey's mom had been coming to church, they had connected more than ever before, and her mom had taken Mrs. Collins to lunch several times, but it wasn't like they'd suddenly become best friends.

"Can I ask you something, Mom?"

"Sure, sweetie."

"Who would you consider to be your best friend?"

Without taking a moment to think about it or look up from the peas she was pouring into a serving bowl, her mom answered. "Your dad."

Amber smiled and had a warm feeling pass through her.

"Why do you ask?"

"I was just wondering. When you said that about being excited Aunt Beth is moving here, I realized you don't have a bunch of girlfriends you hang out with."

"No, I don't," she said. "And you want to know something about why?"

"What?"

"When we first moved out here to the mountains, twenty minutes from the nearest town, we started going to this dinky little church where most of the women were older than me by at least ten years, and I started praying for a really close friend. Back in Tillamook I'd had that. Me and Debbie were almost like sisters. I met her the first Sunday we attended church there, and we were both pregnant with our first baby. Hers was born two months ahead of Ben, and then I had you about the same time she had her second.

"So I asked God for another friend like her when we moved, and I fully expected Him to do it. And I waited, and I waited, and six months went by, and then a year, and I finally broke down one day and cried my eyes out because I felt really lonely, and I couldn't understand why God hadn't answered my prayers. I had friends, but no one like that—someone I could just talk to about anything and have lunch with and share my concerns about my marriage, or my children, or my sometimes unsatisfying career, or my relationship with God, you know?"

"Yes," Amber said, somehow finding it surprising her mom would need that, even though it made perfect sense. She'd never thought about it before.

"And then, just when I thought I couldn't go on another day and I was about to turn my back on God and never speak to Him again for not giving me such a simple request, I heard Him say to me, 'You've already got a best friend right here in your own house, Carol. Someone who's here every single day, and you have dinner with every night, and you talk to all the time about whatever's on your heart; and he's never going to move away, or be too busy to have coffee with you, or someone you have to make an appointment with. And I haven't given you another friend like Debbie because then you might talk to her more than your husband and one day you'd wake up and realize the two of you had drifted apart. And I don't want that to happen, because nobody will ever be as good of a friend to you as he will, and he will never need anybody more than he needs you."

Amber heard the door open and saw her dad enter the house. He was arriving home from work. After removing his coat, hanging it on the peg by the door, and setting his keys on the bench underneath it, he strolled into the kitchen, wrapped his arms around his wife, and gave her a loving kiss.

"Hey, babe. How was your day?" he asked like Amber had heard him say a thousand times before.

"Good. How was yours?"

"Fine, but much better now."

Amber usually turned away when they acted this way, but this time she just watched. They kissed one another affectionately and smiled at each other. Her dad said something loving and sweet, and her mom replied likewise in return.

"Why is our daughter watching us?"

Her mom smiled. "We were talking about you."

"Oh?" he said, shifting his eyes to her for the first time and redirecting his gaze to her mom. "What were you saying?"

Her mom smiled and ran her fingers into his short brown hair above his ears. "I was telling her I'm married to my best friend, and how you're the best answer to prayer I've ever had."

Chapter Two

Amber doubted she had ever been as excited about going to school. Being the first day of the final semester of her high school years was part of it, but she had a far greater reason too. Since Mandy had arrived on Saturday, she had seen her every day, had spent the night with her at Grandma's on Sunday night, and was looking forward to seeing her once again this morning.

Leaving the house thirty minutes before she normally would, she stopped to pick up Mandy on the way, and they entered the front doors of the school with Mandy's class schedule in hand. Amber gave her a quick tour and pointed out all of her classrooms when they passed by. They actually had two classes together: band and history. And when Amber introduced Mandy to Colleen before first period, they discovered Mandy had *AP English, Physics,* and *Calculus* with Colleen, which Amber had suspected might be the case because they were both super-smart.

"Have you ever had that feeling where you know God is so real and so close you can picture Him smiling on you?" Mandy asked both of them as they headed for the band room together.

"Yes," Amber and Colleen said in unison.

All three of them laughed.

"Today is a God moment for me," Mandy said. "How about you guys? When did you last feel that way?"

Amber took a moment to think about it. Colleen answered without hesitation.

"The night I wrote those paragraphs for our *Creative Writing* final."

Amber knew what she was talking about but since Mandy didn't, Colleen went ahead and explained. She had been stressing about what to write and still didn't have anything she was happy with the day before the final assignment was due. Colleen was incredibly smart, but their writing class had been a challenge for her because she tended to think technically about writing instead of letting the creativity flow. She had received a couple of B's on her previous papers and knew she needed to get an A on the final assignment in order to receive one for her final grade. Getting a B in the class would taint her otherwise perfect G.P.A.

Amber had prayed for her and then given her an idea based on something Colleen had shared with her earlier that week. Colleen had always thought of her college plans and future as being something she had to plan out herself rather than letting God guide her, so Amber suggested she write two paragraphs: one describing her feelings of worry, fear, stress, and confusion when she had tried to plan every detail in the past; and a second one describing her current more peaceful feelings once she had decided to wait on God and let Him show her each step she needed to take.

"It was so funny," Colleen said after sharing that with Mandy. "I realized I'd been trying to do the same thing every time I wrote something. Instead of writing from my heart, I was trying to follow all the writing rules that were probably made up by someone who didn't have a creative bone in his body."

They had reached the band room, and Amber took Mandy into Mr. Bolton's office to introduce her to their band teacher rather than having a chance to share one of her many recent God moments.

There was Mandy moving here, of course, which she felt God had surprised her with—like when she suddenly had this boy named Seth in her life. And then when everything had come together concerning her college plans—that had definitely been a God moment she had hoped for but didn't expect to happen like that.

Even some of the low times she had been through during the last few months she could now look at as being God-moments too. Breaking her wrist and not playing volleyball, her grandfather dying, and the Winter Dance not turning out quite like she'd imagined it. God had used all of that to teach her so many things, she couldn't even list them. But above all He had proven His faithfulness and constant presence in her life.

The only thing she felt she was currently struggling with was how to share with others all that God was, and all that He was doing in her life. She could talk easily with people like Seth, Colleen, and Mandy. And she had gotten better about talking with Stacey and Nicole and some of her other friends whom she had become spiritual mentors to. But she never felt like she knew how much to say. She either felt she didn't say enough and should have been more encouraging—or more tough on them if they were making bad choices, or she felt like she was being too preachy and judgmental when they said or did something she didn't feel was right.

But the thing that frustrated her most was her silence when she saw and heard things going on all around her in a public school that were so anti-God she couldn't even believe it, let alone know what to do or say. Seth often told her about times he'd stood up for the truth in class, written something in the school paper, or talked about God to one of his classmates.

And Colleen was really great about stuff like that too. She had invited three different girls to her youth group this year who were now attending on a regular basis. Last year she felt happy about getting Stacey to come to camp with her, but that hadn't happened because she'd made some great effort. Stacey had simply asked her what she was doing that summer, and when she told her she was going to camp, Stacey had said she would like to get away from her mom for a week, and so Amber had asked if she wanted to go with her, and Stacey had said, 'Sure, why not?'

She had also been a good friend to Nicole and helped her to get back to God during a difficult time, but again all she'd done was listen when Nikki had opened up to her and encouraged her to remain with Spencer and come back to church.

Some days she felt like she was doing fine. She had spent her summer working at camp and been a part of many lives being impacted and changed. She'd had little moments of talking with this friend or that one, listening, giving some advice, and praying for them; but she never felt she did enough. For as many opportunities she took to share her faith or say a kind word or be a good friend, there were so many more she missed.

That feeling was magnified that afternoon when she rode with her teammates across town for their basketball game. She sat with Nikki, and Nikki had exciting news to share. Over Christmas Break one of her friends had thought she might be pregnant. Nikki had encouraged her to go to a Christian-based pregnancy center that was in Sandy, just down the street from the high school, and take one of their free pregnancy tests.

"She asked me to go with her, and so I did, and her test turned out to be negative. But while I was waiting for her to finish talking with one of the counselors there, the woman at the desk gave me some information to read about abstinence, and I went ahead and told her I was already committed to that, and then we got to talking and she asked me if I might be interested in being a peer counselor there."

"Are you?"

"I told her I'd think about it, and I've been praying that God would show me if I should. And I keep hearing Him say, 'Yes, Nikki. Do it.' And so I think I'm going to."

Amber smiled and gave her a hug. "That's very cool. I can see you doing that."

"Really? I hope I'm not getting in over my head."

"I don't think so. I remember feeling that way about counseling last summer, but I ended up loving it. I think God gives us what we need when we need it."

"Okay, I'm going to give it a try."

Amber sort of expected Nikki to ask her to go with her and maybe volunteer too, but she didn't. She had often seen the center there on the corner and wondered if she might be able to help out in some way. She knew Kerri spent a few hours a week as a peer counselor at the one Mrs. Kirkwood directed, and she always knew that would be a place she would point any girl at school to who needed to talk to someone, but so far she hadn't felt a strong desire to volunteer—not like she felt about going to camp. And she hadn't been aware of any girls she knew who thought they might be pregnant, so she'd never had the opportunity to be involved in that way either.

Still, she wondered if she should, and she decided to pray about it, but she didn't get any clear direction over the next few days. On Saturday she was able to have the entire day with Seth, but she was feeling a little depressed. She wasn't sure why. It had been a great week with having Mandy here, winning both of their basketball games, and Nikki had told her yesterday afternoon that she had gone back to the center and talked to one of the staff members more about volunteering. She would be starting her training next week. She had even decided to quit her job so she could give as much time there as possible, and Amber was very happy she was so excited about it.

"What's wrong, sweetheart?" Seth asked after they'd had lunch at her house and then settled themselves in the living room to do homework together on the cold and rainy day.

She looked up at him. She hadn't said anything about feeling the way she did, but apparently he'd noticed.

"Nothing," she said. She wasn't trying to hide her true feelings, she just wasn't sure why she felt so low today.

He kept staring at her, but she didn't know what to say. She moved over to sit closer to his side. He put his arm around her and held her against his warm body.

"What's on your mind?"

She thought long and hard about that. What was she thinking? "I don't know," she finally said. "Just sort of blah, I guess."

"About us?"

"No, not about us," she said, draping her arm across his waist and being reminded of how content she felt about their relationship. She had been feeling that way since returning from camp and especially since they had made the decision to attend the same college together and saw God lead them to Lifegate in such a strong way.

"Something going on with one of your friends?"

"No, not really. It's just me."

He waited for her to go on, and she told him what she was thinking.

"I think God might be disappointed in me."

A deep pain entered her heart. Speaking the words seemed to make it true. God wasn't pleased with her, and she couldn't keep the tears from falling.

"What makes you think that?" Seth asked seriously.

"I'm not very—I don't know, fruitful, I guess. I mean I have been in the past. But not much is going on right now. I don't feel like I'm making a difference anywhere, and I'm wondering if I'm supposed to be doing something that I'm not."

"Like what?"

She told him about Nikki volunteering at the pregnancy center and also about her lack of leadership in youth group lately. She felt she should be doing more to get to know and mentor the younger girls, but she didn't seem to be connecting with them very well.

"Is there anything you feel God is definitely asking you to do that you're not?"

"I don't know. I don't know what He wants, and any efforts I do make don't seem to go the way I hope."

Seth held her gently, and she didn't expect him to say anything. This was between her and God, she supposed. Seth certainly couldn't relate to the way she was feeling.

He tilted her chin up and kissed her on the forehead. "You're listening to the wrong voices," he whispered.

"The wrong voices?"

"Yeah, those voices that say, 'You're not good enough; you should be doing more; you call yourself a follower of Jesus?—ha!'

She smiled. "Have you been reading my thoughts?"

"No, I've had them plenty of times myself."

"What's wrong, Seth? Why do I feel this way?"

"Because God is doing a lot of stuff you can't see right now, and because you're forgetting God loves you no matter what—

even if you are doing all the wrong things, which I highly doubt is true."

Amber knew he was right, but she felt lost. God seemed distant. Silent. She didn't like it.

"You know what I see when I look at you, Amber?"

"What?"

"I see a person who loves others easily, and who has joy and peace that spills over to others around you. I see someone who patiently waits for God to do His thing. I see someone who is kind and good and has a gentle spirit. I see faithfulness—to your friends and to God."

"Thank you," she said, generally accepting all that as being true—although she felt she could do better in some of those.

"And you know what all of that means?"

"What?"

Seth smiled and quoted a familiar verse. *"The fruit of the Spirit is love, joy, peace, patience, kindness, goodness, gentleness, faithfulness, and self-control.* You can't be like that on your own. That's the fruit, Amber—what's inside of you. All that God has made you to be as you have been seeking Him."

Amber felt a weight being lifted from her heart, and Seth's final words helped to remove it completely.

"It's not about what you do for Him, it's about what He's doing in you. And just let Him keep doing it, Amber, because He's making your heart more beautiful every single day."

Chapter Three

The following morning at church the youth room was fuller than Amber had seen it for quite some time. Other than on holiday weekends when some of the college students had been home and joined them, they'd only been averaging about ten students with both middle school and high school combined.

But on the cold January morning, even with some light snow falling outside, they had eighteen there, and several of them Amber didn't know. They were all younger than her, mostly middle-school age, and several of them were visitors who had come with friends to the Wednesday night youth group they'd started this month and held at the middle school gym.

That had been a casual time of socializing, eating snacks, playing volleyball or floor hockey, and then having a short devotion time at the end led by her dad. He was very good at talking in a straightforward, non-threatening way about God. He didn't follow a formal lesson or go into deep theological truths, he just spoke about the realness of God and His free love that was available to anyone who wanted it.

He taught in a more structured way on Sunday mornings with handouts and having them open their Bibles and look up verses, but he still kept it casual and relevant to issues they all faced every day—getting along with parents, friendships, handling peer-pressure, and the stress of being a teenager in today's world.

He wasn't the most dynamic teacher Amber had ever heard, but his teaching style kept the interest of everyone most of the time, even the younger boys who had tended to be inattentive and disruptive in the past.

"Thanks for doing this, Daddy," she told him after class. "You're doing a great job."

"You think?" he asked, not appearing too sure about that.

"Yes. Even Kevin and Andy were listening! Now that's an accomplishment."

He smiled at her and looked like he could use a hug, so she gave him one. "Just keep sharing the truth. I always listened to what you told me, and they will too. Maybe not right away, but when they figure out their way isn't working, they'll remember what you said."

"Thanks, Jewel," he said. "I keep trying to tell God I'm not a teacher, but He doesn't seem to be listening."

"You're doing great, Daddy. Don't listen to the wrong voices." She expected her dad to ask what she meant by that, but he didn't.

"Seth was right yesterday, you know."

"Eavesdropping again?" she said in mock disgust.

He laughed. "The acoustics in that living room aren't the best for having a private conversation."

She knew that from previous experience. From the kitchen you could hear everything that people were saying around the corner, but from the living room you couldn't hear a thing—like parents coming inside the front door or down the stairs to grab a snack.

"So what was Seth right about?" she asked. They had talked about a lot of things yesterday, but nothing she wouldn't want her dad to hear too. Seth wasn't the kind of guy to talk and act one way with her and completely different with her parents.

"The part I heard was when he was talking about the fruit being inside your heart. These younger girls in the group look up to you, Jewel. I can see it. They're watching you."

"And that's a good thing?"

"That's a very good thing. You don't have to tell them the truth about God, you're living it, and that's more powerful than any thirty-minute Sunday school lesson will ever be."

Her dad's words remained on her mind for the next hour as she attended the worship service, and she remembered something about her middle-school and early high-school years. Spencer's older sister, Sarah, had played a vital role in her life, she realized. Sarah was two years older than her, and had always been very nice. She had never done anything like leading a Bible study or spending time with her outside of church, but Sarah had taught her a lot about what being a Christian looked like.

Amber had watched her more than she realized until today, and it sent a little chill through her to think that some of the younger girls in the group were now watching her: seeing her at church every week, how she acted at school, the way she was with her friends and with Seth, her actions and attitudes; they were seeing all of it.

Oh, Jesus. May I be a good example for them to follow. May they see my love for You as pure and genuine, and may I be a positive influence in their lives like Sarah was for me. I pray they will come to know you like I know you.

Seth called her that afternoon with some news to share. Pastor John was planning to take a mission team to Mexico over Spring Break, and he had specifically asked Seth if he would go and said she could come too if she wanted.

"I know we talked about going to visit Lifegate then, but when Pastor John asked me today, I had a feeling that I'm supposed to go. I've been a little apprehensive about going because I got sick last time, but I think it's time to get beyond that. If I end up becoming a youth pastor, I'll probably lead teams myself someday."

"I think that's great," she said, feeling a little disappointed they wouldn't be going to visit the college but open to wherever God was leading them.

"Do you think you might like to go?"

"Maybe. How long do I have to decide?"

"Two weeks."

"Okay. I'll think about it. Or do you really want me to go?"

"I'd love for you to go, but you follow God's voice, sweetheart, not mine."

"Do you think there might be another time we could go visit the school?"

"Yes. We'll definitely figure out another time. Do you think your mom and dad would let you miss a day or two of school?"

"Probably. I'll ask."

"Are you feeling any better today?"

"Yeah, a little," she said. "This morning my dad said something that made me realize I'm probably influencing those around me more than I can see."

"He's right. And even if you aren't influencing anyone else, I know for a fact you're making a difference in my life."

"And you're making a difference in mine."

"How do you feel about Mexico?" he asked.

"I said I'd think about it."

"Yes, but you usually have an immediate sixth-sense about these kinds of things. What's your heart telling you?"

"I don't know yet," she laughed. "This is a pretty big deal—going to another country. Honestly it scares me, but I'm not going to make a decision based on that. I have this little thing I do called praying—have you heard of it?"

"Okay, sorry. I'll back off. I'm just feeling really excited about it, and that's a big deal for me."

After he let her go, Amber told her mom and dad about it, and they said it was fine if she wanted to go and thought it sounded like a great opportunity for her. She did run another idea by them she had thought about while talking to Seth.

"Mandy wants to go see the college too, and I had been debating about asking Seth if she could go along with us, but I wasn't sure if they would have room or if Mandy would be comfortable going with a bunch of people she doesn't know. Do you think if I decide not to go to Mexico, we could visit Lifegate that week?"

"I suppose that would be possible," her dad said. "You pray about it and let us know what you decide."

Amber decided not to mention anything about possibly going to Mexico to anyone that week, not even Mandy and Colleen. She felt this was something that needed to be between herself and God, not something she looked to her friends for advice about. On Thursday they had an away basketball game in Portland, and she sat beside Stacey on the bus. Stacey had something to tell her.

"I talked to Paige today about me and Kenny," she said.

"You did?"

"Yes."

"When?"

"At lunch. That's why I didn't come sit with you."

"Did you tell her everything?"

"Yes."

"What did she say?"

"At first she didn't believe me, and then she was mad I've been lying to her. But I didn't care. It felt good telling her the truth."

"I'm proud of you," she said.

"Yeah, right. This is long overdue, Amber."

"That doesn't matter. You're doing the right thing now."

She went ahead and told Stacey about the decision she had to make about the mission trip. Stacey had never been the type of friend to tell her what to do, and she'd had enough time to think about it on her own to know how she was leaning.

"So, you don't think you're going?" Stacey said after she had more or less told her that's how she felt.

"I don't think so," she said. "I don't feel God leading me there at this point. I'd actually like to go with Seth, but I think that's the only reason I'd be going, and I'm not sure that's what I should be basing it on. I'll probably tell him tonight."

She didn't say anything else, and Stacey didn't comment either. They talked of other things, including how Stacey was feeling about getting married this summer. She was still undecided, but she and Kenny had both sent in applications to be at camp this summer, and they would be making their final decision by Spring Break.

Seeing Seth at the game was nice. He hadn't been able to come to many of her basketball games because of his swim schedule, but this week his meet wasn't until tomorrow. They sat together during the JV game, and he didn't wait too long before asking her if she had thought any more about going on the mission trip, and she could tell by the way he asked that he really wanted her to go.

"Give me a few more days," she said, not wanting to tell him what she was truly feeling. She didn't know why God would be telling her no. It didn't make any sense. And she began to wonder if she was as close to God and following Him as well as she thought.

On the ride home from the game, she worked on her homework on her laptop and then wrote more on her novel she had begun three weeks ago. She had written two full chapters so far and was almost done with the third. Since she was basing it on someone she knew well, she didn't have much trouble getting started. She had talked to Stacey about it and asked if she would mind her writing a story similar to her and Kenny's real-life one, and Stacey said, "If you can write a story about my sorry life and actually get people to read it, you really are gifted."

But Stacey's pessimism hadn't deterred her in the least. If anything, it only made her want to write it more and show Stacey her life was worth telling about. It was something younger girls and those their own age could learn from.

"Did you tell Seth you're not planning to go to Mexico?" Stacey asked on the drive home after they returned to the school.

"Not yet."

"He really wants you to go, doesn't he?"

"How do you know that?"

"Just in the way you said that."

She sighed. "Yes, he does. I was going to tell him, but then I decided to pray about it a little more. It doesn't make any sense for me to say no."

"Aren't you the one who always says that sometimes the things God wants us to do don't make sense, and that's where faith comes in?"

"Yes."

"Have you asked God for clear direction?"

She laughed. She always asked Stacey that when she was debating about a decision. "Yes."

"And do you feel like you're getting it?"

"Yes."

"So, what's the problem?"

Amber laughed again. Stacey loved to mock her in a loving way. She did the same, arguing back the way Stacey usually did. "I don't know," she whined. "How can God's voice seem so clear and so vague at the same time? Can't He come up with a better system?"

Chapter Four

Over the course of the next two days, Amber continued to waver back and forth about her decision concerning Mexico. When she had seen Seth on Thursday and could tell he wanted her to go, she'd felt torn between what she felt God was telling her and Seth's obvious wishes, and that didn't change by the time she saw him again on Saturday afternoon.

She decided not to mention it. She had another week to decide. Seth didn't say anything about the trip either, but it was on her mind throughout the afternoon. God seemed to be leading her to remain behind and go visit the college campus with Mandy instead, but she knew going to Mexico to do some good work was a great opportunity and she felt guilty about not going. She continued to wonder if she was listening to her own desires or God's.

On Monday she told Colleen about it, and her reaction was similar to Stacey's. "You're asking me? Now that's a switch."

"What would you do?"

"I'd do what God was telling me, even if it didn't make sense. I've done that plenty of times, and I know you have too, and it always works out fine, right?"

"Yes, and I do feel at peace with God, but not so much with Seth. I don't want to disappoint him."

"Amber. If anyone will understand and accept it when you say, 'I don't think God wants me to go.'—It will be Seth."

Amber knew she was right, and she felt better, but by the end of the week she began to dread seeing Seth and having to tell him she didn't want to go. She was never like that with him, and the unsettled feelings she'd been having about herself continued to escalate. On Friday they were going to visit Ben and Hope at college, and Amber knew she could use a good talk with her brother about this.

Stacey and Nicole went too. Spencer came up from Eugene to spend Friday evening and Saturday with Nicole, but Kenny was in Arizona this weekend for baseball. His first game of the season had been last week, and he would be away for several weekends in a row as they played games in the warmer climate areas before having games up here where Stacey could go and watch.

Spencer and Nicole seemed very happy to see one another, and Amber felt amazed things were going so well between them, and especially for the changes she could see in Nikki. She knew she shouldn't be amazed. This was what she had prayed for.

Nicole was currently looking into what college she wanted to go to. She was leaning toward a local Christian college more than a state school. She had always done better when she was surrounded by others who shared her faith and were constantly watching out for her, and she knew she would need that in college. Spencer had made it clear he wanted their relationship to continue and said she didn't need to worry about him losing interest or latching on to some other girl if she decided to go somewhere besides the University of Oregon with him.

Amber had a special reunion of her own, not only with Ben and Hope, but also with Lexi, whom she hadn't seen since the end of the summer. They had been writing to each other regularly, so they were pretty up-to-date on each other's lives, but it was good to see her face-to-face again. She and Josh were still together, and Lexi was happy with their relationship. Her mom hadn't been doing so well, however, and Lexi said having Josh as a close friend to lean on had been helping her through the difficult months.

They stayed in Hope and Lexi's room that night. She and Stacey shared a large air-bed, and Nicole had a single-sized one for herself. They stayed up late and talked about a lot of different things, including their plans for the summer. No one knew about the possibility of Stacey and Kenny getting married except for her and Seth. Kenny called Stacey when he got to his room after the baseball game, and Stacey stepped out to talk to him. Amber knew she had really been missing him the last few days.

Amber got to see Lora the following morning, and Eric came to meet her after they returned from breakfast. Amber had seen them together at Kyle and Julia's wedding two months ago, but there was a definite difference in the way they looked at each other and interacted now. They were engaged, and it showed. Eric greeted Lora with a much more affectionate kiss than she had ever seen him give her before, and it made Amber feel so happy for Lora. She had been through so much but taken the risk of loving again.

It was a cold and rainy weekend, so they went bowling after lunch and then went to see a movie before having dinner. She hadn't had a chance to talk to Ben much, at least not privately, and she was about to give up on that possibility when he pulled her away from everyone after they returned to his dorm.

"Are you okay?" he asked, sitting beside her on a sofa in the corner of the common area. "You seem a little down today."

She didn't respond. She felt the same about the trip as she always had, but she didn't understand why.

"All right," he said, crossing his arms in front of his chest. "What did Seth do?"

She smiled. "Nothing. It's not him, it's me."

"What's wrong, Amber?"

She told him everything. He asked if she felt afraid to tell Seth she didn't want to go, and she answered honestly.

"No. I know he won't try to pressure me into it even if he feels disappointed, but I'm not sure I'm making the right decision. I don't know what to do."

"Have you talked to Seth about any of this?"

"No."

"Why not?"

"I don't know," she whined. "I feel indecisive, and I don't like it."

"Talk to him, Amber. Aren't you the one who tells me how he always says the right thing?"

"Yes. But I feel like this should be my decision."

"You can talk to him and still make your own decision."

Amber took Ben's advice and asked Seth to go for a walk with her. She was supposed to be giving him her decision by tomorrow, and she felt stupid for waiting until the last minute to share her honest thoughts, but once she got started, it all came out easily, and she waited for Seth to speak his mind.

"I don't want you to go for me, Amber."

"I know you don't," she said, "but I'm not sure what I'm supposed to do. Maybe I should go. How am I supposed to know?"

"I think you know."

"But how can that be right? Why shouldn't I go to Mexico and spend a week sharing about Jesus and helping to build a house for a poor family?"

"Because that's not what God has for you right now."

"But why not? You're going. I could go too. The only thing that's stopping me is me deciding not to go."

"But I don't think you're deciding. Jesus is."

"How do you know?"

"Because I know you, Amber. You know how to listen to God. I've been watching you do it for a year and a half."

She felt better and knew Seth was right, but some of the unsettled feelings remained. Seth hugged her and held her close. "It's fine if you don't want to go," he restated. "I trust your decision one-hundred percent."

"You're not mad?" she asked.

"No, of course not."

"Do you think God is?"

He stepped back and looked at her. "Do I think God is mad at you?"

She nodded and felt tears welling up in her eyes.

"Oh, sweetheart," he said, holding her close once again. "Of course He's not mad at you. Why would you even think that?"

She couldn't respond. She didn't know why she felt this way, but she did. "What if I'm faking it, Seth? What if I think I'm on the right path, but I'm really not? What if I think I'm making the right choices and doing the right things, but it's only because everything He's asked me to do has been easy, and now that the hard stuff is coming, my faith is crumbling to pieces?"

He took a moment to respond, but the words he spoke were the truth, and she recognized that immediately. "If you're wrong, Amber, about this or anything else, His mercy covers it. His great love for you covers everything. Not just blatant disobedience, but also mistakes and bad decisions and discovering that you're deaf and blind when you thought you were doing fine."

"Ben was right."

"About what?"

"That you would say the right thing."

He laughed. "Ben said that?"

"I guess he's finally believing everything I tell him about you."

"And what do you tell him?"

"That you love me, and treat me right, and he doesn't need to worry."

"And you know what God tells me about you, Amber?"

"What?"

"That He loves you very much, and that He has great plans for you because you listen to Him and go where He leads—and only where He leads. He doesn't have to shout with you, Amber. You hear Him whisper."

She and Stacey and Nicole were planning to go to Lora's apartment tonight, and she knew they should be heading there soon. She hoped to have some good time to talk to Lora, but she also wanted a few more minutes with Seth. After two weeks of feeling not quite herself around him, it was nice to have everything feel right again. It was always hard for her to receive his affection freely when she had other things on her mind.

"I was thinking of asking Mandy to go with me to see the Lifegate campus that week," she said. "My mom and dad said they would drive us down there. Is that okay, or did you really want us to go together?"

"No, that's fine."

"Are you sure?"

"Yes, and I think I may know one reason why God doesn't want you to go on this trip, Amber."

"Why?"

"They can only take a certain number of people, and when Pastor John asked me to go, I immediately asked if you could go too, and he said yes. But you going might mean someone else can't who's really meant to be on that trip. And I've been thinking the last few days that if you decided you didn't want to go, I would encourage Matt to go instead. He needs it much more than you do, Amber. Trips like this usually impact those who go just as much, if not more, than those we are going to help."

Amber smiled and felt better. And she immediately began to pray that Matt would go in her place. He had been doing well since December, and Seth was trying to get him to go to camp this summer and to Lifegate next year, and she could see how a trip like this might lead to the other two.

"I'm sorry I placed this kind of a burden on you, sweetheart," Seth said, now with tears in his eyes. "I should have prayed about it before I asked you."

She smiled and hugged him. "Yeah, and then I probably would have been mad you were going without me."

He laughed.

"God's grace covers your tiny little faults too, sweet thing."

With a much lighter heart, she said good-night to Seth before she headed to Lora's apartment along with Nicole and Stacey. Lora was currently living by herself in the one-bedroom, off campus place she had shared with Julia during Fall Term, so Amber took the empty bed in the bedroom and Nicole and Stacey slept in the living room.

She and Lora stayed up late. She told her about things going on in her life: youth group, her relationship with Seth, their decision about college, and their plans to return to camp this summer.

Lora talked about her student teaching she was currently in the middle of, and a few other things, but mostly she talked about Eric. It was obvious to Amber she was very much in love with him and felt confident in his love for her.

"I almost cried when I saw the two of you together this morning," Amber said. "Not because of everything you've been through, but at the way Eric looked at you and kissed you right in front of everybody. I've never seen him kiss you like that."

"I know. It's weird. He's still the same Eric I fell in love with and dated for two years, but he's also different. He decided he didn't want this thing between us to be a part of his life, but for it to be the absolute center. I'm not sure why, he just did."

Amber smiled at her. "You want to know a secret?"

"What?"

"Last summer when I found out you and Eric broke up and I talked to Seth about it, he said he wasn't surprised because of things he'd heard Eric say about not wanting to bring a woman into his life until he knew what he was doing with his future."

Lora smiled. "And what did your incredibly insightful boyfriend have to say about that?"

"First he told me he didn't feel that way about us. He thought it was okay for us to have a serious relationship and we shouldn't be afraid of it, because as long as we seek God first and let Him guide us, He will always show us the right way."

"And?"

"He also told me if I was going to pray and ask God to bring the two of you back together, I should pray for Eric to stop trying to control his life at every turn, let God lead, and realize *you are* the most important part of his future."

Lora stared at her. Tears welled up in her eyes, but she didn't speak. Amber got out of her sleeping bag to give her a hug.

"I'm so blessed to have him, Amber. He's such a special person. Thank you for praying for us and telling me to give it another chance."

"God led me to, Lora. I know it. He brought you together, and He wants you to have a happy life, full of special times and for a special purpose."

Chapter Five

On Sunday afternoon Seth drove to Portland and took the three of them to the MAX station to catch a train to Gresham. Amber gave him a long hug and told him she would be praying about Matt possibly going on the mission trip in her place.

As soon as she got home, Amber called Mandy and talked to her about going to visit the Lifegate campus over Spring Break, and Mandy thought that sounded fun. She told her about the weekend and asked Mandy about hers. Originally she had invited Mandy to go along, but Mandy had a youth group activity with her church on Saturday she had opted to go to because she was trying to get to know everyone there better.

"This guy sort of asked me out," she said, sounding uncertain if she was happy about it.

"Sort of?"

"He doesn't believe in dating, and so he asked if I could come over to his house sometime for dinner to get to know him and his family."

"Who is he?"

"His name is Michael. He's a senior, but he doesn't go to Sandy. He's homeschooled, and he's also taking classes at community college this year."

"Do you like him?"

"I don't know. He's at church every Sunday and Wednesday, and he's talked to me, but I just thought he was being friendly. On Saturday he spent almost the whole time with me and then asked about having dinner with them on the ride back to the church."

"Are you going?"

"We haven't set an official time. He's going to call my dad sometime this week and set it up."

"Are you excited?"

"I don't know. I'm not sure if he really likes me or if he's trying to figure that out. I'm not sure what to expect."

Amber had heard of guys who approached relationships in a more traditional courtship way instead of modern dating, but she didn't have any friends who had been involved in that kind of a relationship.

"I guess you'll find out," she said. "He sounds like a neat guy if he's that concerned about where and when you spend time together."

"Yeah, I think he is. Grandma knows his family pretty well, and she said they're a nice family. But it's a little intimidating for me to be around a lot of people I don't know well, and I have the feeling I'll be the center of attention at dinner."

Amber laughed. She could relate. She remembered when she met Seth's family for the first time, but she had gotten to know Seth pretty well by then, so that had helped.

"I'll pray for you," she said. "And don't worry about being anyone but yourself. If he's the right guy for you, it will work out fine, and if he's not, then it doesn't matter. God will bring him along at the right time and in the right way for you."

"You want to know something funny?"

"What?"

"Ever since I've been seriously thinking of going to Lifegate with you, and especially since moving here to where I basically don't know anyone, I've been thinking I don't want to date until at least next year because I don't want to meet someone here and then have to be away from him when I go to college."

"And now God is bringing someone along when you least expected it?"

"Yeah, sort of. Although when Michael asked me, I wasn't as excited about it as I always imagined I would be. I don't know if that's because of the way he's approaching it or if it's because I'm not really interested in him, you know?"

Amber thought of her own experience with Seth. He had approached her in a somewhat similar way by asking her dad for permission to come see her sometime, and their early dates had been more family-centered than the way she had imagined her first dating experience would be, but no matter how Seth had approached it, she felt certain her reaction would have been the same. She had a definite interest in him and would have gone to his house for dinner or to the moon for their first date if he would have asked.

"Go with your heart, Mandy. God is there. He'll let you know if it's right. Don't be afraid to stick with it if you're enjoying yourself or to walk away if it's not working for you."

"Don't be with him just to be with somebody; is that what you're saying?"

"Yes. No matter what package it comes in, I think you'll know when it's right."

"Was there ever a time you weren't sure if you wanted Seth in your life?"

"No. I wondered if he wanted me in his life, but I never had a moment where I said, 'I'm not sure if I like this guy or not.'"

"Okay. I'll keep that in mind," she laughed. "To be honest I felt that way a few times on Saturday, but we'll see if that changes."

Amber had homework to finish before Bible study, and when she was done she had a half-hour to write more on her novel. Hearing Stacey telling Lora recent details of her relationship with Kenny this weekend had given her inspiration to keep writing, and she had to tear herself away to make it to Bible study on time.

That evening their lesson was on listening to God, and she was able to share the decision she had made about not going to Mexico and realizing that sometimes God doesn't lead us the way we think He will or in the way that makes the most sense. She also shared about how God had given her peace in knowing that even if she wasn't hearing right and making the wrong decision, His grace would cover it.

On the way home Stacey told her she had been feeling that way about getting married this summer. She didn't think it was the right time, but she was afraid of Kenny being disappointed and making the wrong decision and losing him over it, or waiting too long to get married and spoiling the purity of their relationship.

"Kenny loves you, Stace. Believe in that love. He's going to understand, and if you're following God's voice, it can be nothing but good."

"But why is God telling me and Kenny different things?"

"Maybe He wants Kenny to be ready to marry you at this point, but He wants you to think about what you really want and yet have the security of knowing Kenny isn't going anywhere."

"I was going to tell him this weekend when he called, but then I couldn't. Do you think it would be okay for me to tell him over the phone, or in a letter?"

"When are you seeing him again?"

"Not for three weeks. If I'm going to tell him, it would be better sooner than later, and I'm not sure I want to use the one day I have with him that weekend. I'd rather tell him now."

"I think whatever you do, it will be fine, Stace. Kenny loves you."

They had reached her house, and Stacey leaned over to give her a hug. Stacey still wasn't much of a hugger, but she had grown into it more over the last year.

"Thanks, Ambs. Thanks for always being here for me. I'm going to miss you next year."

Amber smiled. "Then come to Lifegate with me instead of going to OSU with Kenny."

She laughed. "I'm not going to miss you that much."

Amber told her good night and got out of the car. Ascending the steps and entering the house, she was greeted by her dad who said Seth had called a few minutes ago and wanted her to call him back. She did, and he had exciting news to share: Matt had said 'yes' immediately when Seth asked him about going to Mexico, and he had also filled out the application for camp.

"I think Stacey and Kenny might be going too," she said, going on to tell him what Stacey had told her tonight. "Do you think that was the right advice for me to give her? If it was you, would you rather have me tell you in person?"

"Maybe, but I would understand if you needed to tell me in the way you were most comfortable with. I think it'll be all right. I don't see their relationship going down the drain over it."

"Me neither."

"Do you still have homework? Should I let you go?"

"No, I finished this afternoon and then I worked on my story. But I had to stop in the middle of a scene to go to Bible study, so I'd like to finish that before bed. I have a hard time getting any writing done during the week."

"Are you happy with it so far?"

"Yes. It's coming easier than I thought it would, but I'm sort of learning as I go along. I'm about halfway through that book you gave me. It's been really helpful."

"I'm glad. That's why I got it for you."

"Thanks for believing in me. I'm not sure I would be doing this otherwise."

"I do believe in you, Amber. I'll let you go finish that."

"Okay. Thanks for a great weekend too. I'll miss you this week."

"And I'll miss you. See you on Saturday."

"Okay. Bye."

"Bye, Amber. I love you."

***

Amber had a good Monday and Tuesday, but Wednesday was a bit of an emotional roller-coaster. It started out great. It was Valentine's Day, and Seth had left a gift for her with her mom, so she started the day by reading a sweet card and finding another bear inside the gift-sack to add to her collection. This one was bright red and it played the theme from *Swan Lake.*

Stacey picked her up for school, and the day went downhill from there. Stacey had mailed the letter to Kenny before leaving her house. She said that was the hardest thing she'd ever had to do and wasn't sure what Kenny's reaction would be. Amber tried to be supportive, but Stacey wasn't too consolable, so she mostly left her alone on the drive. But then when she got to school, she had a very nervous Mandy on her hands. Michael had called her dad last night and arranged to have her over for dinner on Friday, which she thought was fine, but she wasn't too sure about having to see him tonight at youth group.

"How should I act, like we're together, or like we're just friends?"

"Be yourself, Mandy. I know I keep saying that, but that's all you can do."

"But what if he tries to hold my hand or something?"

Amber laughed. "Do you want him to?"

"I don't know," she whined. "How did I get myself into this?"

They needed to get to class, so Amber gave her a hug and told her they could talk about it later. "You still have ten hours before you have to see him. He obviously likes you. Now all you have to do is spend time with him and see if you like him back."

That afternoon she had a letter waiting for her from Seth, and she decided to read it before dinner instead of waiting until bedtime like she sometimes did. She had been feeling much better about her decision to not go to Mexico since hearing Matt would go in her place, but Seth's words were encouraging also.

Dear Amber,

I've been thinking a lot about what I said to you on Saturday about God's grace covering everything—from minor mistakes to major acts of disobedience, and I witnessed a good example of this yesterday. I'm sure you remember Erin from the dance. She went with Pete that night out of pure ignorance. She had no idea of the kind of guy he was, and she accepted a seemingly innocent invitation to the dance from him. It wasn't like she deliberately went with a guy she knew wasn't a good choice, and yet she ended up having a really bad night—except for one thing: She met Kerri.

Last night at youth group Erin gave a brief testimony about how much her relationship with God has changed and grown during the past two months, and she credited Kerri for being such an encouraging mentor to her. But if she hadn't gone with Pete that night, she may still be stuck in what she called 'A very blah relationship with Jesus.'

I know you see me as someone who is solid with Jesus, and I am, but you are a big part of that, Amber. I truly believe God brought you into my life as a way of drawing me closer to Him. I've thought a lot about what you said, and I realized that in many ways I'm feeling like you do about being afraid God is disappointed in me, but I've been keeping myself too busy to think about it. I know we can't earn God's love, but sometimes I live like I can. Please pray for me in this. I think I need to slow down a little and get refocused on my relationship with God more than what I'm doing for Him.

I love you so much, sweetheart. I don't know what you see when you look at yourself, but I see someone who is so honest and real—with God and others, and especially me. That's a rare quality I appreciate about you very much. All you have to be for me is exactly who you are, and I know God feels the exact same way.

All my love,
Seth

Chapter Six

Amber called Mandy after dinner to let her know she would be thinking of her tonight and praying. She had managed to get her to relax somewhat during the day, but she sounded tense again.

"You don't have to go to youth group tonight," she said, just now thinking of that. "You could come out and go to mine with me."

"Could I? Really?" she asked, sounding like she had been thrown a life preserver in a raging river.

"Sure," she laughed. "Make him wonder about where you were. Maybe he'll call you tomorrow."

"Do you think I should go?"

"I think you should do whatever you want to do. If you really don't want to see him tonight, then don't. You'll probably have a difficult time focusing anyway. Come have fun with me, unless you're missing him terribly."

"Not really," she said, laughing mildly. "Do you think that's a bad sign?"

"Just give it a chance, Mandy. You won't know until you give it a try, unless you seriously don't like him already."

"No, I like him. He's nice and everything, but I don't know him very well yet, and I'm not sure I'm ready to be around him right now. I'll come out there as soon as we finish dinner."

"Okay. See you."

She hung up the phone, and it rang almost immediately. It was Seth. He didn't have a lot of time to give her because he had leadership team tonight, but he wanted to call and let her know he was thinking of her today. She thanked him for the bear, and he thanked her for the card she had sent him. She had a gift for him too but planned to give it to him this weekend.

"You're my best friend too, Amber," he said.

The card she had sent him said that, along with a lengthy note she added including all the reasons why. She said it once again over the phone, but in a different way.

"I'm really happy Mandy and some of our other friends might be going to camp with us this summer and to Lifegate next year, but if I could only pick one person from my high school years to have with me into college and beyond, it would be you, Seth. No contest."

"Me too, baby."

"Really?"

"Yes, really!" He laughed. "I'm not letting you go, Amber."

She smiled. "Actually, I'm feeling very emotionally stable right now—secure in our relationship and about the future. Are you feeling that way too?"

"Yes."

"Do you think that's because we don't have any major struggles right now or because we're on the right path?"

"Both. We're avoiding a lot of potential struggles by being on the right path, but God is carrying us through these months that could be stressful, but they're not."

"That's what I was thinking this morning when I did my reading: Like God is shining a strong beacon of light on us and everything seems so clear and right."

"Nothing but blue skies, you mean?"

She smiled. "Yes, exactly."

Mandy came out and went to youth group with her that evening and decided to spend the night also. She seemed relieved about not having to see Michael, but she did tell her more about him before they went to sleep—what she liked and what she didn't. Amber didn't say anything, but she had the feeling this wasn't the right guy for her cousin. He seemed too serious for her. Mandy needed someone fun and spontaneous who would make her laugh, not make her feel stressed. Someone who made her smile when she talked about him.

Both Stacey and Mandy seemed better on Thursday, but on Friday they were both a mess again. Kenny hadn't called last night, so Stacey was certain he hated her, and Mandy wanted to back out of her dinner-date with Michael but knew she couldn't. Amber had tried to encourage them and give them advice on Wednesday, but when her similar words didn't seem to be having much effect as they ate lunch, she told them she wanted to pray for them. Colleen and Nicole were there too, and the five of them had a spontaneous prayer-time together in the noisy cafeteria, and Amber didn't know if the others felt it, but she had an amazing sense of God's presence surrounding them.

Not just because of the prayers they were saying for one another, but also because of the way God had brought the five of them together and how much their relationships with God and one another had grown in the last year. After spending the majority of her freshman year without any close friends, and only having Colleen her sophomore year, Amber knew only God could have done this—for her and for them.

On Saturday morning she called Mandy at eleven, and her cousin said the dinner had gone okay. She still felt unsure if she liked Michael in that kind of way, but she said it hadn't been horrible. More fun than she thought it would be. She liked his family, but she didn't feel completely comfortable with Michael yet.

"He's coming over to my house for dinner next Friday," she said.

"Did you invite him?"

"He suggested it, and I said okay. I do want to get to know him better. I think I got to know his family last night more than I did him. I'm not sure he's the easiest guy to get to know. Did you feel that way with Seth at first?"

"Not really. I know what you should do."

"What?"

"Ask him to write you a letter."

"Yeah?"

"When you see him at church tomorrow, ask him, okay? And then tell him you'll write him one back. That's how Seth and I got to know each other quickly in the beginning. It's easier to say what you're thinking on paper than face to face with someone you're just getting to know."

"Okay, I'll ask him," she said. "Why does this dating stuff have to be so complicated?"

"You're not dating, you're courting."

"Dating, courting, whatever! Is it really worth it? Am I ever going to find my Seth, Amber?"

"Of course you are. Michael might not be him, or maybe he is."

"But how am I supposed to know?"

"I think you'll know. I can't explain it, but I did."

She tried calling Stacey after talking to Mandy to see if she had heard from Kenny, but no one answered, so she worked on her book and did homework. She had noticed snow falling earlier, and by the time she finished her reading, she could see it was starting to pile up. She hoped Seth wouldn't have any trouble getting out here. He had worked today and was supposed to be here by two-thirty. They usually kept the highway clear, but if it was icy too, that could be dangerous.

By the time he arrived at three o'clock, she was a nervous wreck. She stepped outside the front door but waited on the porch for him. The steps were covered with a thick layer of snow.

"Sorry I'm a little late," he said, carefully navigating the stairs to reach her. "It was really coming down in town, and there was a minor accident blocking traffic."

She hugged him when he reached her and held on tight.

"Hey," he said. "I'm here."

"I was getting scared."

"I'm here," he repeated, giving her a tender kiss. "I'm sorry, sweetheart. I should have called. Forgive me?"

"Yes," she said. "I'm just glad you're here."

He kissed her again. "And I'll be here until Monday night."

Monday was President's Day so they had a three-day weekend, but right now having extra time with him didn't seem like enough. "No! I don't want you to ever leave again."

He smiled. "Guess what?"

"What?"

"I broke my own record in the 100 on Thursday."

"You did?"

"Yep, and you know what else?"

"What?"

"There was a guy there from the University of Oregon, and he offered me a full-ride scholarship to swim for them."

"He did?"

"Yes. And he told me in four years he could turn me into one of the fastest freestyle swimmers in the world."

Amber stared at him. Why was he smiling like that? Was he considering taking it?

"And you know what I told him?"

"What?" she whispered.

"I said I was more interested in going to the right school for me and my girlfriend than being a world-class swimmer."

"You did?"

He kissed her tenderly. "Of course I did. We're in the homestretch now, baby. I'm not going to be away from you any longer than absolutely necessary."

"And how long is that?"

"112 days."

She smiled but wondered if Seth was making this decision too quickly. "You turned down a scholarship for me?"

"No. I turned down a scholarship for us."

He kissed her again, for much longer this time. Neither one of them heard her dad sneak up on them until he started whistling and began shoveling the snow off the front steps.

Amber giggled and peeked around Seth's shoulder. Her dad looked up and winked.

"Hi, Daddy. Seth's here."

"I see this snow didn't stop him from getting to you. I was going to shovel it off earlier, but I thought I'd leave it and see if he turned around and went home instead of risking a broken leg."

"Oh? Is it snowing?" Seth asked. "I hadn't noticed."

Her dad smiled. "It's pretty cold out too, but I'll bet you didn't notice that either."

"No, not really," Seth said.

"I do have a nice warm fire going inside if you're interested," he said. "But if not, Mrs. Wilson and I will make good use of it and you can stay out here."

"Now that you mention it, I am feeling a little cold," Seth said. "How about you, sweetheart?"

"Yes, I think so. Thanks, Daddy."

"You're welcome, Jewel. Tell your mom the snow has stopped falling for the moment and we can go for that walk she's been pestering me about all day."

"Okay," she said, opening the door and stepping inside the warm house. Her mom was at the table working on her Sunday school lesson for tomorrow, and Amber informed her of Daddy's invitation.

Her mother smiled and didn't hesitate to lay down her pen and get up from the chair. The phone rang at the same moment, and Amber answered it while her mom went to put on her boots and warm coat. It was Stacey.

"Hey, Stace. I tried calling earlier but then I forgot to try again. Have you heard from Kenny?"

"Yes, he called me this morning," she said.

"Is he still speaking to you?"

"He was disappointed when he got the letter, and he didn't want to call me right away and try to change my mind, so he waited until today and called me from California. We talked for a long time."

"About what?"

"About going to camp this summer and getting married next year."

"Yeah?"

"Yep. You okay with that?"

"You know it."

"Is Seth there?"

"Yes."

"Can I talk to him for a minute?"

"Sure," she said, wondering why, but she didn't ask. "See you tomorrow?"

"Yes. We should be there unless this snow gets any deeper."

"Okay, bye," she said, handing the phone over to Seth with a shrug of her shoulders.

Seth took the phone from her and said hello to Stacey. Amber couldn't tell what Stacey had to say by anything Seth said except for at the end: "You're welcome, Stacey."

He laughed at something Stacey said and then told her good-bye and hung up. Amber had settled herself on the couch in front of the fire and waited for Seth to join her.

"What was that about?"

"Kenny called me on Thursday, and she wanted to thank me for what I said."

"Kenny called you?"

"After he got the letter. He wasn't surprised or upset, but he wanted to talk to me about how he could ensure their relationship remains pure for another year, especially once they're living away from home on a college campus together."

"What did you tell him?"

"Basically what we've talked about before with asking Jesus for help, and for Kenny to see it as his way of showing Stacey love by protecting their relationship. He was thinking of encouraging Stacey to either remain up here for college or to come with us to California, but I told him I didn't think that was the right solution. Avoiding tempting situations can be helpful, but it's not fail-safe, and that's something we can do in our own strength. It's not about that. It's about believing and trusting God, not just avoiding the issue."

"Is that what Stacey was thanking you for?"

"Yes. She's been counting the days just like we have."

Seth began kissing her then, and since her parents had gone for a walk, they were alone in the house. But she didn't feel the need to stop him from giving her the sweet affection. That's what Seth's kisses were to her: very sweet and loving. And with the advice he had given Kenny this week, she knew the commitment he'd made to her and the way he managed to keep it was fresh in his mind.

"Do you still like my kisses?" he asked.

"Yes."

"As much as always?"

"More," she said. "The more I get to know you and the closer I feel to your heart, the more I enjoy them."

He reached for her wrist and held it gently. Her gold heart bracelet had become her favorite piece of jewelry she had ever owned—for its meaning and the beauty of it.

"You know that hug you gave me when I got here today?" he said.

"Yes."

"I liked that. It made me feel like you need me."

"I do, Seth. Anytime I think about something happening to you, I go absolutely crazy. I don't worry about much anymore, but that's one thing I don't know if I will ever be at peace with—of losing you in a tragic way."

"Don't worry about it, Amber. God knows exactly what you need. If that's me, then I'll be here. I can't promise you nothing will happen to me, but I can promise as long as I'm here, I'm yours. I have no desire to be away from you or to be with anyone else, and I can't imagine that changing."

There was no doubt in Amber's mind he meant that, and she felt the same way about him. She had wanted to be with Seth as much as possible from the beginning, and that desire only increased as the months went by—nearly eighteen now.

He kissed her again, and she felt thankful Seth was always strong about showing her his affection without going too far, because she felt weak.

"I love you, Amber," he said, pulling her close to him and just holding her.

"Am I still your best friend?" she asked, not because she doubted it, but because she wanted to hear him say it.

He laughed. "Unless God Himself takes you away from me, that position has been permanently filled."

Chapter Seven

"Hey, guess what?"

Amber took her eyes from the winter wonderland scene surrounding them. After her parents had come back from their walk, Seth had asked her if she wanted to go for one before they lost daylight.

"What?"

"Kerri has a date tonight."

"She does? With who?"

"I don't think you know him. He's in our youth group, has been for years, but he's quiet and hasn't been an active part of things until recently. I think he's always had a good relationship with God, but connecting with people hasn't come as easily. He went on the six-week mission trip to Mexico last summer, and that brought him out of his shell. When we got back from camp and saw him again, it was like he was a totally different person."

"Is Kerri excited?"

"I think she's curious," he said, smiling at his sister's defining characteristic.

Amber laughed. She could imagine Kerri being curious about a guy who had once been shy and reserved but now brave enough to ask one of the most beautiful girls in his youth group out on a date. Seth and Kerri's birthday had been earlier this month, so Kerri was eighteen now, the age she had wanted to wait until going out with anyone.

"Do you think he was waiting for her to turn eighteen?"

"Yes. He told her that when he asked her. And technically it's not a date," Seth said. "He asked if he could court her."

Amber gasped. "That's what Mandy's doing! A guy in her youth group talked to her last weekend about courting her, and she had dinner at his house with his family last night."

"How did it go?"

"Okay. She had a nice time, but she's not sure about Michael yet."

"Kerri knows Dylan pretty well. After he talked to her, Kerri told me she's had her eye on him since school started. He's a neat guy. He was before, but now he's letting others see that more."

"What are they doing tonight?"

"His family is going to a dance performance his younger sister is in. He invited Kerri to go with them and then afterwards they're going out for dessert."

"I'm excited for her, are you?"

"Yes. I think this could be a good thing. And even if things don't work out on a long term basis, Kerri will enjoy spending time with him."

"What makes you think it won't work out?"

"It might, but Kerri's only reservation about starting something with him is he's going to Guatemala this summer and she's going to camp, and then he's planning to go to George Fox for college. But I told her that can change. Falling in love with someone has a way of changing our independent plans."

Amber laid her head on Seth's shoulder and enjoyed his closeness as they walked through the white powder at their feet. She said a silent prayer for Kerri to have a good time tonight and get to know Dylan better than Mandy seemed to have gotten to know her courter last night.

“I’m glad you got to know my family so well when we first started dating,” she said, realizing how true that was. “At the time I didn’t think about it, but it made a big difference. Did you plan that, or did it just happen?”

“I didn’t think about it beforehand so much, but when I decided I wanted to let you know how much I wanted to see you again, I knew I should see if meeting your parents was a possibility. The only explanation I have is that God led me to, because it wasn’t something anyone had taught me and certainly not the most comfortable thing to do.”

“I’m glad I asked you to come to my birthday party. At the time I was thinking of an excuse to see you again, but I look back now and see it was a great way for you to meet my family and for them to get to know you. You talked to my mom and dad that day even before you talked to me!”

He laughed. “I know. And I didn’t plan that either.”

“That’s God’s grace, isn’t it? Neither of us had a clue what we were doing, but God brought it all together in just the right way?”

“Yes, I’d say so.”

Amber sighed. “I’m having a God moment.”

“A what?”

Amber smiled. She had gotten used to Mandy saying that and forgot Seth wasn’t familiar with the new lingo. “A God moment: When you see God working in the details to bring everything together so perfectly.”

Seth stopped walking and turned to face her. “Oh, a God moment: Like when I came across this hurt girl in the woods that I had been thinking about all week?”

“Yes, like that—only this is a God moment I’m experiencing over something that happened a year and a half ago.”

They were both silent for a moment and then Seth spoke again. "You know what I've come to see as a God moment from our early days that I didn't realize until this summer?"

"What?"

"How open you were with me from the beginning. How you opened up your heart to me. At the time I thought that was just who you were, but seeing you around a bunch of people you didn't know this summer—especially the other guys who were there, I saw a different side of you. The side that loves and accepts others easily, like you did with me, but who also guards your space. I never once saw you return any of the attempts other guys made to connect with you."

She laughed. "I didn't know they were trying."

"I know. That's the beauty of it. Somehow you responded to me doing the same kinds of things, but you were oblivious to it with everyone else. I know there were guys who liked you before I came along, but you didn't notice—like when you never had a clue Adam was interested in you until he asked you out."

"I thought that was me being naive."

"I don't think so, Amber. God opened your eyes to see me, and He opened my eyes to see you—the one He made for me."

Amber got chills, and it wasn't from the snow that was beginning to fall once again. She had been feeling very secure in their relationship since returning from camp and especially since deciding to go to the same college and seeing God bring all the pieces together. But now, hearing Seth say how God had opened his eyes to see her, she saw herself as being wrapped in the grace of God like a cozy blanket, and she felt one-hundred percent at peace with her relationship with Seth and her life as a whole.

"Grace and peace to you," she whispered.

"What?"

"It's a verse," she said. "Mandy wrote that to me in a letter after she found out she was moving here, and I have it on my wall, but I didn't get it until now."

Her mind shifted to Mandy then, and she realized what was likely missing in her cousin's experience with Michael. Her eyes were not open to him. He was doing everything right—approaching her in a respectful, honorable way; He was a nice guy, a Christian from a good family; Well-mannered; Close to God. But he wasn't the one for her. Mandy's eyes had not sparkled when she talked about him. She hadn't wanted to see him on Wednesday night and not much more on Friday.

Amber didn't think it had anything to do with Mandy's natural shyness. She would open up to the right guy, and he would open up to her—without effort, without careful planning, with or without the perfect conditions. He would see her whether she was dressed in her most perfect outfit or with Pepsi spilled on the front of her clothes, and she would see him whether he asked her to have dinner with his family or asked her out to the movies.

She decided not to tell Mandy any of that yet. She would wait and see how things played out in the coming days. Maybe Mandy's eyes would open to see Michael in a different light after spending more time with him, but she had her little speech prepared for when Mandy said to her, 'Why isn't it working? What am I doing wrong? He's a great guy; Why don't I see him the way you see Seth?'

They turned around and began walking back to the house with the snow beginning to fall more heavily. "I think your dad has better timing than me," Seth laughed. "He took your mom for a forty-five minute walk, and I got ten minutes."

"He knows these mountains better than city-boys."

"Well, I got forty-five minutes with my girl in front of a cozy fireplace, but he is going to be rudely interrupted much too soon."

The following morning they went to church. The snow had piled up quite a bit during the night, but her dad's truck didn't have any trouble making it through the packed snow in their driveway, and the highway had been mostly cleared by early-morning snow plows.

Stacey and her family were there, and they all went out to lunch together at a nearby restaurant. Stacey came over to the house to hang out with them afterwards. It was obvious she missed Kenny, and Amber knew these last few months of school were going to be the most difficult for her with Kenny's busy baseball schedule that had him tied up every weekend. It made Amber feel more thankful for the time she had with Seth, even if it was limited.

Thinking again of what she and Seth had talked about yesterday, she knew Stacey and Kenny's eyes had been open to each other long before either of them knew what they were doing or how to make it last, and she wondered how Kerri's "date" had turned out last night.

"You should call Kerri," she said to Seth.

"Why?"

"To find out how it went. Let her know you're thinking about her."

"How do you know I'm thinking about her?"

"Because I know you, and because it's not every day your sister goes out with a guy."

He didn't deny it and went to make the call. Amber followed him to hear the report, but Kerri didn't answer her phone. He called the house and talked to his mom and then told her what he knew.

"She went out to lunch with his family after church and then they were going to study at his house. Mom said she thought she had a good time last night."

Amber decided to call Mandy. Her cousin had likely seen Michael at church this morning. She usually saw Mandy on Sundays, but they had decided not to go into town to have lunch with them because more snow was supposed to fall this afternoon.

She got straight to the point, and so did Mandy. "He held my hand during church, and I didn't like it."

"Why not?"

"I don't know. I just didn't. I felt like we were on display, like he's trying to force something between us that isn't there."

"Did you ask him about writing you a letter?"

"No. I was going to, but then I didn't even want one."

"It's okay to end it, Mandy. Just call him and say you would rather be friends."

Amber knew what Mandy was thinking.

"There will be other guys, Mandy: The one who's right for you."

"But what if I'm giving up too soon? He's a really nice guy, Amber."

"Then God's grace will cover it. Michael will pursue you relentlessly until you see his charm in all its glory, and you'll love him more than you ever would have before; or something will happen to bring you together down the road; or you'll miss him terribly by Wednesday and go running into his arms at youth group."

They both laughed.

"I think I'll give it one more week," she said. "Will you come to dinner on Friday so you can meet him and tell me if you think I should stick with it?"

"Sure."

"You will?"

"Yes. If you want me to."

"Thank you," she said. "I'm so glad I have you to share this with. I was so stressed-out ten minutes ago, but now I feel better."

Amber smiled. "It's not just me. Grace and peace to you, Mandy, from God our Father."

Chapter Eight

After dinner that evening, Amber and Seth wrote a letter to Jonathan together, the boy they were sponsoring in Columbia through Compassion, and then they filled out their official applications for Lifegate that were due by March 1st. The first part was pretty basic: standard information about who they were, where they lived, SAT scores, GPA's, and extracurricular activities. But the remaining pages reminded Amber of the application for Camp Laughing Water. She felt comfortable sharing about her personal beliefs and reasons for wanting to attend Lifegate and felt confident she was writing what they were looking for, but she had some apprehension about getting accepted, just like last year when she had applied to be on staff at camp.

"Has Kerri sent hers yet?"

"Not yet. She's still praying about it, hoping to get some kind of confirmation from God like we did."

"How will you feel if she ends up not going?"

"I want her to do what's right for her, but I'll miss her. Other than you, she's the best friend I've ever had."

"Who would you consider to be your best guy-friend?"

"Right now, or ever?"

"Both."

"Probably Matt, but Chad is a close second, especially during this past year."

"How is Chad? I haven't heard you talk about him lately."

"He's good. He's very focused right now with school and looking for direction for his future, and his relationship with God has become more solid and personal. It seems like all we talk about is God. I never imagined that."

"Has he applied to Multnomah?"

"Yes, but he's thinking about a few other colleges too, including Lifegate."

"Would you like to see him go with us?"

"Sure. I think it would be great, but I'm not trying to push him into anything. He's learning to let God lead him, and I don't want to interfere with that."

"Is he still interested in Jessica?"

Seth smiled. "Oh, yes."

"Are they both going to be at camp this summer?"

"I don't know. Chad's about eighty-percent sure he wants to go back, but I don't know about Jess."

Amber began to think about the possibilities of who might be at camp this summer and at Lifegate in the fall. At this point it could be quite a few on both counts, or it could just be her and Seth. She would have included Kerri in that a week ago, but now with Dylan entering the picture, she could imagine Kerri changing her plans.

On Monday they went snowboarding with Chris and Colleen. During one of their breaks where they hung out in the mountain lodge together, Amber asked Colleen if she had decided about the retreat coming up in a few weeks. It was with Seth's youth group, and Amber knew she was going for sure, but when she had talked to Colleen about it, she said she would have to check her schedule—which meant checking with Chris' schedule. Since Colleen had quit her job a few months ago, they'd had a lot more time together, but Chris' hours were still long on some weekends.

"Oh, I forgot to tell you," Colleen said. "I'm going to Arizona a week early."

"Before Spring Break?"

"Yes. One of my cousins is getting married, and my mom really wants to go, so me and her are flying down on Friday—the same weekend as the retreat, and then my dad and brothers will come the following weekend."

"You're missing a whole week of school? You can barely stand to miss one day when you're sick."

"I know," she laughed. "But I talked to my teachers, and they agreed to give me the assignments early so I can turn them in after Spring Break and make up any tests, and I think it will be fun to go with just my mom and have that time with her."

Amber looked at Chris. "And how do you feel about her being gone for two weeks?"

"Well, since I'm going to be gone for eight this summer, I guess I can't complain too much."

Amber thought of her own separation from Seth that she would be enduring over Spring Break also. They were going on the retreat together, but then she wouldn't see him for three weeks because the team would be leaving for Mexico the following Friday and not return until Sunday afternoon a week later. Seth had told her he could see her that Sunday, but she knew he would be tired and could use the day to rest, so they wouldn't be seeing each other until the weekend after he returned. They'd never gone that long without seeing each other, but knowing they only had two more months of week-long separations to endure after that, she supposed she could survive.

Since Colleen couldn't go on the retreat with her, Amber decided to ask Mandy, and Mandy said she would. On Friday night she went to her grandma's house after basketball practice, arriving about an hour before Michael was coming for dinner. Both Amber and Mandy helped Aunt Beth with making dinner, and Mandy seemed relaxed as they both changed into dressier clothes.

"I'm not as nervous about him being here as I was about going there. And having you here makes me feel better," Mandy said. "Thanks so much for doing this."

"That's what friends are for," she said.

"Do you really consider me to be a friend, Amber, not just your cousin?"

"Of course I do," she said, giving her a hug. "You're one of the best friends I've ever had."

When Michael arrived, Amber waited in the living room along with Mandy, Aunt Beth, and Grandma while Uncle Tom went to answer the door. He chatted with Michael for a moment and then led him to where they were all waiting. Amber's initial impression of Michael was favorable. He was polite, and it was obvious he really liked Mandy. He had brought her flowers, and when she rose to meet him, he gave her a sweet kiss on the back of her hand.

Mandy introduced him to everyone, even though he already knew Grandma and her parents from church. Michael took note of the resemblance between herself and Mandy, saying something sweet about them having too much beauty in one family.

Dinner was pleasant enough, but watching Mandy and Michael interact with each other, Amber could see what she had suspected about Mandy's eyes not being open to Michael. Mandy seemed to have an okay time, and Amber thought she might agree to see Michael again if he asked, but after Mandy came in from saying good night to him on the front porch, she informed her otherwise. He had asked her about doing something on Sunday after church, and she said no, that she would rather be friends and only see each other at church and on youth activities.

"I'm proud of you," Amber said, giving her a hug.

"Do you think I made the right decision?"

"I think so. It's better to be honest than fake it."

Two weeks later they went on the youth retreat with Seth's youth group and Amber was excited about going with Mandy. They had never done anything like this together before. She also felt she could use a good spiritual pick-me-up before being away from Seth for the next three weeks.

Friday night was fun, and they went to bed late. They were dragging a bit on Saturday morning as a result, and it rained most of the afternoon, forcing them to remain indoors during much of free-time. They hung out with Seth and his friends, playing card games and singing karaoke in the cafeteria. When the guys decided to go play football in the muddy, rain-soaked field, she and Mandy went back to the cabin to do homework. Kerri came in awhile later, and Amber had the chance to ask how things were going with Dylan, who was here this weekend.

She had seen them together several times between last night and today but hadn't been able to determine if Kerri was seriously falling for him, although Dylan seemed to be quite taken with her. He was nice, and Kerri seemed comfortable around him, but not all that different than the way she was around her other guy-friends.

"It's going okay," she said. "He's definitely worth getting to know better, and I have a good time with him, but I'm not speculating one way or the other at this point. I'm trying to focus on the friendship and letting whatever happens, happen."

She had only come to the cabin briefly to change out of her jeans that had gotten wet when she and Dylan had gone for a walk in the rain. She was going to be meeting him in the chapel to go over their lines for a short play they were in tonight. Seth had written it and asked them to play the lead roles.

After she left, Mandy got very quiet, and when Amber noticed, she asked her what she was thinking about.

"Michael."

"Do you miss him?"

"No. Not at all."

"So what's wrong?"

"Why don't I miss him? Why didn't it go that way for me?"

"Go what way?"

"Like the way Kerri and Dylan are seriously getting to know each other. I feel like I didn't give it a chance."

"When you want to give something a chance, you will."

Mandy didn't seem convinced. Amber sensed there was more going on than Mandy was telling her. "What else are you thinking about?"

Mandy lifted her eyes briefly but didn't answer.

"Mandy! What?" she laughed. "Tell me!"

"Nothing."

"I'm not buying that. Come on, spill it."

Mandy was lying on her stomach, and she propped herself up on her elbows and spoke adamantly. "You can't tell anyone this, not even Seth. Can you promise me that?"

"Yes."

"Not even Seth, especially not Seth," she insisted.

"I promise, Mandy. What?"

"There's someone here I'm very attracted to, and that hasn't happened since I've reordered my priorities about the kind of guy I'm looking for."

"And you feel different about him than you did about Michael?"

"Yes. Way different."

"Who?"

Mandy hesitated but then went ahead and told her—sort of. "I sat by him at breakfast this morning and across from him while we were playing cards this afternoon."

Amber replayed both scenes in her mind, and she smiled. "Matt?"

Mandy smiled sweetly at the mention of his name. "Yes," she whispered.

"What's wrong with that? Why are you even thinking about Michael?"

Mandy's sullen look returned. "Because," she said. Tears welled up in her eyes and she looked away.

"Because why?"

"Because I can never have someone like that."

"Like what?"

"Extremely good-looking, popular, funny. No offense Amber, but he's even better looking than Seth!"

Amber laughed. She did think of Matt as being a very attractive guy—not the one for her, but definitely one of the cutest guys she'd ever met. "What makes you think you could never have him? You don't know that."

"It's not going to happen. I know it. It's completely impossible. And I'm thinking, 'How can I turn someone like Michael away who's actually interested, and instead have these crushes on guys who are out of reach?"

"You can't force yourself to like somebody, Mandy. I didn't have to decide if I was going to like Seth, it just happened."

Mandy didn't respond. Amber asked her something else.

"What do you like about Matt? Besides the obvious."

"I don't know, just something about him. The way he acts. The way he treats people. The way he looks at me."

"How does he look at you?"

"I don't know. I can't explain it, but there was a moment this morning at breakfast, and several while we were playing cards when he looked at me and I felt the world stop, you know?"

"Like when you both reached for that spoon and grabbed it at the exact same time and neither one of you let go?"

Mandy smiled. "Yes. He winked at me and said, 'I'll arm-wrestle you for it,' and I didn't want to let go—not because of the game, but because I didn't want him to look away. It was like we were the only two there."

Her eyes are open to him!

Amber kept the thought to herself. Only time would tell if Matt felt the same way about her, which she thought was entirely possible. "He is a cutie, and he's very sweet."

"He makes me smile," Mandy added.

"Let me tell Seth, and he can set up a double-date for us like he did with Chris and Colleen."

"No! I don't want Matt to feel like he's being set up. I want him to pursue me like Michael did."

"Maybe if he knows how you feel, he will."

"Amber. You promised me."

"I know, and I won't say anything. I'm just saying it's possible, Mandy. I know for a fact Matt is looking for a girl exactly like you."

"How do you know?"

"Because he told Seth he's looking for a girl like me, and we're not that different, Mandy. And you're cuter than me with that ultra-slim waist and those great blue eyes. You're smarter, you're sweeter, and I can see you with Matt every bit as much as I see myself with Seth."

"But the reality is I'm not, Amber, and I never will be."

Amber left her alone at that point. Sometimes the more she tried to cheer Mandy up, the more depressed she got, and Amber knew there was nothing she could do about Mandy's feelings for Matt anyway. She wasn't going to say anything about it to anyone, and she couldn't force Matt to like Mandy. She didn't think it was impossible, but she also didn't have any reason to believe Matt had seen her cousin in the same way as Mandy saw him.

She did watch Matt for any signs of attraction to Mandy when they sat with Seth, Matt, Kerri, and Dylan at dinner, but she didn't see any obvious signals. He did talk to her several times, but not more so or any differently than anyone else. Matt had a natural friendliness about him and was often the center of attention, and Amber had no doubt many girls looked at him the same way Mandy did. If she had experienced a unique connection with him that really meant something, Amber had no way of knowing. The thought they both may be at camp this summer and at Lifegate for the next four years made her believe the potential was there for something down the road if nothing happened right now, but she kept all of that to herself.

That evening everyone gathered in the main room to sing and listen to the speaker, and then later they returned to see the play Seth had put together, listen to students perform musical talents, and hear testimonies. Because of the play, Seth, Kerri, and Dylan were backstage when she and Mandy were finding seats, and Matt ended up sitting beside them. They had saved four seats, and at first Matt sat beside her, but then he got up and said, "I guess I'll let Seth sit beside you, and I'll go over there."

Amber watched him step past her and sit beside Mandy instead, and Mandy glanced at her, but Amber didn't do anything to give her secret thoughts of excitement away. Matt started talking to Mandy, and Amber didn't interfere. Seeing the two of them together like this instead of in a group setting made Amber see something in Matt's eyes that was different than before. And even though she was sitting there too and Matt knew her better, Matt's attention was more focused on Mandy.

She couldn't be certain, but she had a feeling Matt's eyes were open to Mandy too.

The play was very good, and Amber was glad she hadn't asked Seth about the premise beforehand because her ignorance made her see the unfolding of events the way everyone else did, and it had a touching message about true friendship. Kerri and Dylan and the other actors did a nice job. Seth had written and directed it but didn't play a part himself. She had learned earlier he had originally given himself the part that Dylan played opposite Kerri but then he asked Dylan to take it to give him and Kerri more time together, and also to help Dylan with coming out of his shell more. He said a year ago Dylan would have never done anything like that.

Following the play, they learned Pastor John had asked several people to share about specific things God had been doing in their lives. One girl shared about how God had completely changed her view of Him during the last few months, and she sang a song that expressed how she had come to know Him.

As others shared their talents and special words, Amber was encouraged and feeling close to God, but then another guy shared, and she lost some of that. He talked about how for a long time he had played games with God, acting like one person at church and then another at school. That had changed for him when one of his friends had been seriously hurt in a car accident earlier this year and he'd come face-to-face with the reality of death. The fact his friend could have died that night without knowing God hit him hard. He'd never taken the time to invite him to youth group or shared about his own beliefs in any way.

His friend had come to know Jesus after that, and he was here at the retreat with them. Amber was happy to hear the news, and it reminded her of her own experience with helping

Stacey to know God, but it also reminded her she hadn't been doing much lately to share Jesus with others she went to school with. A deep feeling of failure and guilt entered her heart, and the guy's closing words didn't help.

"If you can relate to what I'm saying about not being completely committed to Jesus, stop thinking about yourself. Look around you. People are dying—physically and spiritually, and we're the only ones who can save them. God is counting on us, and we're letting him down."

Chapter Nine

Pastor John ended the evening by talking about specific ministries within the youth group they could be involved in. Amber knew he wasn't talking specifically to her because she didn't go to church with Seth, but she did feel there were a lot of things she could be doing in her own youth group and at school that she wasn't.

They left the meeting with instructions to go to the cafeteria for a late night snack and participate in a karaoke contest, or they could go to bed. She told Seth she was tired and left the room with Mandy, feeling very depressed.

"You told Seth, didn't you?"

Amber snapped out of her private thoughts. She didn't know what Mandy was talking about. "Told Seth what?"

"That I like Matt."

"No."

"Then why did he sit by me?"

"So I could sit by Seth. Or maybe because he actually likes you."

Mandy let it drop, but Amber knew she didn't believe her. She had *déjà vu* of a similar time in the eighth grade when Nicole had accused her of telling their friends a secret about the guy she liked.

"I didn't, Mandy. I promise."

Amber vowed to herself she wasn't going to even hint about it to Seth or anyone else, which she hadn't planned on doing, but she knew it could come out sometime if she wasn't careful. The romantic side of her wanted to try and get them together in a fun, teasing-like way, but Mandy was sensitive, so she needed to be careful about stuff like that. And she also knew if it was meant to be, God didn't need any of her silly scheming to make it happen.

Half of their cabin went to bed, and the other half straggled in over the next hour, with the majority of them coming after the karaoke contest was over. Apparently Kerri and Dylan had won. Amber had gotten into bed, but she was wide awake until long after everyone was in their beds and the cabin was quiet. She finally opened her heart to God in the darkness and told Him what she was feeling.

I know I'm failing you, Jesus. I act like I have it all together, but I really don't. I should be doing so much more for you, but I'm not. I'm caught up in my own interests, in my relationship with Seth, in my plans for the future, and I'm ignoring the dying world around me. I've been a pathetic student-leader in youth group lately. I haven't led anyone to you since last summer at camp. I couldn't even make a commitment to go to Mexico for a week because I want to go visit a college campus instead. And I'm messing with other people's lives when I have no idea what I'm talking about: giving Stacey advice about getting married, and telling Mandy to give up on Michael just because she didn't have stars in her eyes like I did with Seth, and thinking I want to marry Seth and be by his side in ministry. I'm not who he thinks I am. I'm going to hold him back.

I can't do this, Jesus. I can't follow you. It's too hard. I'm not who you need me to be. I'm just going to keep disappointing you. I'm never going to be strong enough. I should give up now—stop playing games with you and everyone else. Seth would be better off without me. I don't deserve him.

She almost got her iPod out of her bag to listen to music. That often helped when she was feeling down about something, but she couldn't bring herself to listen to someone singing about God right now. She longed for the encouragement but didn't think she deserved that either.

On Sunday morning she went through the motions of greeting Seth in her usual way, singing and listening during the morning meeting, acting like she was fine, but inside she was dying, and she had no idea what to do about it.

For the first time in a year and a half, she began to think about breaking up with Seth. She wasn't the right girl for him. She didn't deserve him. Somehow she had blinded him to who she really was. When he saw her, he saw someone else. Someone much better than who she really was. She had fooled herself into believing she had a special relationship with God, but she obviously didn't.

She didn't want to go to camp this summer. She didn't want to go to Lifegate. She could only pretend better in places like that. It was time to give up the pursuit of a God she could never please and would only continue to disappoint. It would be better to be honest with herself and everyone else and turn her back on Him than to proclaim to love Him when she really didn't.

If she loved Him, she would be doing so much more. She would be committing every waking minute to Him and be like that guy who had started an on-campus Bible study at his school this year, or that girl who had decided to go on a year-long mission trip to Russia following graduation, or the one who had hosted a weekend slumber party for her entire basketball team, took them to church with her on Sunday, and led three of her teammates to Christ on Sunday afternoon. Those were the kind of servants Jesus was looking for, and she was completely pathetic in comparison.

"You okay, sweetheart?" Seth asked after they had gotten into the van and were waiting for it to head out.

"Yeah, fine," she lied, giving him her best smile.

"Did you have a good weekend?"

"Yes. I think Mandy did too. Thanks for inviting us."

They were sitting in one of the middle seats of the van, but Mandy was in the front passenger seat because she tended to get carsick on winding roads like the one leading to the camp. Seth leaned over and whispered something in her ear.

"Does Mandy like Matt?"

Amber knew she would give the truth away if she didn't answer immediately. "Not that I know of."

Seth took her word for it and didn't try to push it or say anything about Matt liking her. She felt bad for lying like that, but she didn't have much choice. Fortunately Seth was in a talkative mood, and he talked the majority of the hour-long drive back to Portland. She listened and pretended everything was fine. Doing otherwise would only lead to him asking what was bothering her and then trying to convince her she was wrong, like he'd often done in the past.

But she wasn't wrong this time, and she wasn't going to give him the chance to tell her otherwise. He only told her what she wanted to hear, not the truth. He loved her too much, and that was one more way she was bringing him down.

Seth drove her and Mandy to the MAX station after they arrived at the church. They had a few minutes before the train arrived, but with Mandy standing right there, Seth didn't kiss her except for when it was time for them to go.

"I'll call you," he said.

"Okay. Bye."

"I'll miss you."

She let the tears fall then. He wouldn't question them now. "I'll miss you too."

He kissed her briefly but affectionately. "I love you. I love you. I love you."

She allowed herself to look into his warm brown eyes, and the words she spoke were the absolute truth. "I love you too."

Mandy didn't question her tears on the way home. Knowing she wouldn't be seeing Seth for a week often brought them on, let alone three. "I'm sorry about what I said last night," Mandy said after they were well on their way.

"About what?" Amber asked.

"Accusing you of telling Seth I liked Matt. I know you would never do that."

"Actually, I might," she said, thinking of how she'd had to lie to him earlier. "It's hard for me to keep stuff from him, but I'll try hard. I promise."

"Well, it's not like I'm going to be seeing Matt again anyway, so I suppose it doesn't matter. I just didn't want him saying anything to Matt while we were there."

"You might be seeing him again. I told you he's going to camp, didn't I?"

"Yes, but I think I'm going back to Cold Springs this summer."

Amber wasn't surprised to hear her say so. Mandy was the type of person to go where she felt most comfortable, rather than someplace new, but Amber had thought she could talk her into going to Camp Laughing Water since she and Seth would be there, but apparently not. And since she wasn't going to camp this summer herself now, Amber supposed it didn't matter, but she couldn't resist sharing something with Mandy she obviously didn't know.

"Matt's going to Lifegate too."

"He is?"

"Yes," she laughed, seeing the look of horror mixed with delight in Mandy's eyes. "A lot can happen in four years."

That was the one bright moment of her day. Once she was back home, her thoughts of self-scrutiny only got worse, and before she went to sleep, she decided what she was going to do. Seth was leaving on Friday with the mission team. She was going to write him a letter this week, telling him she wanted to break up with him—that she had been wanting to for awhile but hadn't had the courage to say so. She would send it next Monday, and the letter would be waiting for him when he got home, and being on a spiritual-high from all the great stuff they had accomplished in Mexico, he wouldn't let her pull him down any longer. He would respect her wishes to not call or come see her, and the loss would cause him to cling to God more and go on with all the great plans God had for him.

She would lie to everybody else too and tell them she didn't love him anymore. That she wasn't ready for a serious relationship. That she had only let it go on so long because she hadn't known how to end it.

She gave herself another day to think about it, but on Monday night before she went to sleep, she wrote the letter. It was a complete lie, but she knew this was the only way. Telling Seth the truth would only lead to more years of pretending. He would convince her God loved her, and she was tired of hearing that. He didn't. He couldn't possibly. And even if He did, she didn't love Him back, not really, so what did it matter? She was tired of living a lie.

She sealed the envelope and didn't look at the letter again, leaving it on her desk with his address and a stamp on it until the following Sunday. All week she had felt determined to send it, and she hadn't read the letters Seth had sent to her. She had placed them in the shoe box under her bed unopened. He'd called her on Thursday night, and she had tried to act normal, blaming any tears or hints of sadness on how much she missed him and would continue to miss him while he was gone.

She wasn't lying about that. She did miss him terribly, but she had shut down her own feelings on this. This wasn't about her. It was about doing what was best for Seth and everyone else—including God. She felt certain Jesus would rather have her get out of the way of all the great things He wanted to accomplish. If she wouldn't be obedient, someone else would be.

She only faltered on Sunday evening when she gave in and read the letters Seth had sent her that week, just to make sure there wasn't something she needed to know before sending her own letter. His words weren't any different than normal, but they were enough to make her cry. Recalling a letter he had written to her several weeks ago after she had been feeling this way about herself, she searched the box and found it. At the end it said:

> *I love you so much, sweetheart. I don't know what you see when you look at yourself, but I see someone who is so honest and real—with God and others, and especially me. That's a rare quality I appreciate about you very much. All you have to be for me is exactly who you are, and I know God feels the exact same way.*

No! That isn't true. He needs and deserves so much more than I will ever be!

On Monday morning she put the letter in the mailbox before they left. Knowing Seth wouldn't actually be reading it for another week helped her to keep her emotions in check on the long drive down to northern California. They arrived in a town near the campus by nightfall, but they stayed in a motel overnight and went to visit the campus the following day.

It was really beautiful, and she liked the dorm room they were able to see. She had been looking forward to this for so long, and she could picture herself living and going to school here with Seth and Mandy and Kerri and whoever else, but at the same time this little voice kept saying, 'It's not gonna happen, Amber. You don't deserve to go to a school like this. You don't belong here.'

Amber hoped her decision to not come here in the fall wouldn't keep Mandy from coming. She would know Kerri and Seth, and Matt. But Amber had already vowed to herself she wasn't going to try and push Mandy into anything. She was done with trying to give others advice about how to live their lives when she couldn't even live her own right.

She broke down and cried that night, but her period had started that day, so she used cramps as an excuse for her tears, and everyone left her alone to rest. She cried for an hour while they were at dinner. She missed Seth so much, and she felt so alone and worthless. She felt like she wanted to curl up and die.

They drove through The Redwoods and stopped along the beach the following day, which were both breathtaking, and then they drove down the coast and spent Thursday in Santa Cruz, riding the rides on the Boardwalk and enjoying the wide, sandy beach on the sunny day.

"I bet you wish Seth was here," Mandy said, walking beside her along the gentle surf. "This would be so romantic."

Amber had a mental image of herself and Seth walking along this beach together sometime in the future, and of Mandy and Matt following close behind: hand in hand, stopping to share sweet kisses. The thought brought a smile to her face and tears to her eyes. Tears for herself and Seth and what would never be, and tears for Mandy and Matt and what might. She could picture them together but wondered if it could seriously happen. Matt was a popular guy who could have any girl he wanted. Would he take the time to notice her shy cousin? And if he did, would Mandy open up enough to let Matt past her quiet exterior?

Amber had brought her laptop along, but she hadn't written much this week except for a little more on her story on the drive down to help the time pass. She had given up her dream of being a novelist as well—of anything like this ever making a difference for anyone. It was just a smokescreen for some nobler pursuit of what she should really be doing. But she couldn't help but write for herself a bit. She enjoyed it if nothing else. It was a selfish thing, but she couldn't seem to be anything else these days.

After Mandy's comment and the mental picture of seeing her and Matt together, she couldn't help but write about it that evening: two people who had met briefly one weekend and then were reconnected several months later on a beautiful college campus near the beach. The girl didn't think she could attract someone like that, so she didn't even try, but she thought about him constantly and her heart beat faster every time she saw him. Amber was only able to write the first chapter that night, but she had the entire story in her head.

They had driven to Sacramento after dinner and were staying in a hotel along I-5 for the night before their long drive home tomorrow. She missed Seth so much. This was the longest she had gone without seeing him for quite some time. She had enjoyed the trip with Mandy and her parents, but she knew it would have been better with him.

"Are you okay, sweetie?" her mom asked the following day before they stopped for a picnic lunch overlooking Shasta Lake. Her mom had let Mandy sit in the front seat as they'd headed into the mountains. Amber looked at her mother, but she didn't respond.

"What's wrong?"

Her dad interrupted, saying they were almost there and asking her mom where she had put the sandwiches they had picked up earlier. "In the small cooler, or the bigger one?"

"The small one," she said. "And it's right here, so you don't have to unload everything to get to it."

Her dad turned and smiled at her mom, tossed her a sweet wink, and said, "Love you, babe."

It was enough to send Amber over the edge.

Chapter Ten

Amber had been feeling numb these past two weeks. She had shut down her heart, ignoring her true desire to have Seth for the rest of her life. She had convinced herself she was of no use to God and could walk away from Him, but she couldn't, and the pain of being a failure returned in full force. She couldn't love Him right, but she couldn't not love Him at the same time. The same was true for Seth. She was at the end of herself and drowning, with no idea how to rise to where she'd once been.

She started crying, and her mom took her into her arms. When they arrived at the picnic area, Mandy and her dad got out of the van and left them alone. She knew her mom expected an explanation, and she wanted to give her one, but she didn't know where to start. Should she lie and tell her mom what she had told Seth in the letter about not wanting their relationship anymore, or should she tell her the truth about why she had written it in the first place?

"I know you miss, Seth," she said. "But is there something else?"

She could lie to Seth in a letter, but she was terrible at lying to someone face to face, and she didn't even try. "Something happened on the retreat, and I don't know what to do about it. I'm so confused."

"What happened?"

"I came away feeling like I shouldn't be with Seth, and I shouldn't go to camp this summer, or to Lifegate, and I ended up writing a letter to him, telling him I want to break up."

"When?"

"Before we left. It will be waiting for him when he gets home."

Her mom repeated her question. "What happened, Ammie?"

She couldn't answer. She didn't know how to phrase it.

"Did something happen with Seth?"

Amber knew what her mom meant by that. "No. It's not Seth. Nothing happened. It's me. I don't know who I am, Mom. I know who I'm supposed to be, but I don't think I can ever be that person."

"What person?"

She told her about the testimonies she'd heard that night, and about the great play Seth had written, and how she felt with him going on the mission trip without her, and how her own efforts lately seemed so pathetic.

"People are living in darkness because I'm not bold enough or doing enough to share Jesus with them, but I don't know how to change that. I shouldn't be working at a place like Camp Laughing Water or going to a great Christian college or dating someone like Seth. I should admit I don't love God like that and stop pretending I do."

She wasn't crying anymore. She was beyond crying about this. It was time to face the harsh reality and admit her failure to everyone.

"So, I'm breaking up with Seth," she said matter-of-factly, folding her arms in front of her chest. "I wrote him a letter, telling him that's what I want, although I sort of lied about why, so I'm going to write him another one, but it's over, Mom. I'm ending it, and I'm not going to camp, or to Lifegate. I'm going to get a job after graduation and move out as soon as I have enough money, and stop wasting everyone's time."

"And then what?"

"I don't know. Just live until I die, I guess."

"And you're never going to let anyone love you? You're going to stop letting God love you?"

"Yes. That's what I'm going to do, and you can't change my mind."

Her mother laughed.

"I'm serious, Mom! I've thought about it a thousand different ways, and this is the only solution. I'd rather be honest about who I really am than pretend to be someone I'm not."

"There's a slight problem with that plan, Ammie."

"What?"

Her mom reached out and cradled her cheek in her palm, waiting for her to look up.

"You can't stop others from loving you."

She let that truth sink in a bit. Her mom kept talking.

"You can't stop me or your dad, or Ben. You can't stop Seth and your other friends. And most of all, you can't stop God. We'll all go right on loving you, but you won't be experiencing it with us."

She hadn't seen it as pushing everyone's love away from her. It was about trying to run from herself, but both were impossible, she realized.

"Love isn't about what we deserve, Ammie. That's what Jesus is all about. He died for us when we didn't deserve it. He did it because He loves us and He wants us to receive that love. It's grace, Ammie."

"But I need to love Him, and I don't know how!"

"Seth?"

"No. God! I don't know how to love Him right. It's too hard."

She started crying again. Her mom moved closer and wrapped her arms around her.

"He wants you to love Him for your benefit, sweetie, not because you're supposed to."

It's all about you, Amber. Let Me love you and trust that I do. That's what I want. Trust Me. Believe Me. That's how you love Me.

Her mother's calm words confirmed the ones she felt God speaking deeply to her heart. "He wants our love because that's the only way we can fully experience Him. And the way you do that is you keep on believing what you already know to be true: that He loves you no matter what. You focus on your relationship with Him, first and foremost—even above serving Him, and you go where He leads *you.* God wants you to know Him, Ammie, not just do stuff for Him. We're not slaves. We're His children."

A lightness began to settle over her heart. Something that had been missing since last weekend. She felt like a child who could live in the freedom of God's love with no strings attached, and she felt perfectly calm for a moment, but then she remembered the letter.

"What am I going to do about the letter I wrote to Seth?"

"When is he getting back?"

"Sunday."

"We could find out when his plane is coming in and go meet him at the airport, and then you could tell him all of this before he has a chance to read it."

"Really? Could we?"

Her mom smiled. "Sure. I was half-expecting you to ask if we could do that anyway."

She asked her mom something else. "Why do you think Seth loves me?"

"The same reason as God. He just does, and you don't have to doubt it. You belong to him."

She gave her mom and hug and thanked her. They got out of the van and went to have lunch with her dad and Mandy, who were patiently waiting for them at a picnic table.

"You all right, Jewel?"

She received the hug he offered her. "Yes, Daddy. I just forgot who I was."

Mandy rose from the bench and gave her a concerned hug too. She knew her mom was right about not being able to stop everyone from loving her, and she felt very blessed to have her family and friends, and she couldn't wait to see Seth.

Once they were back on the road, she did her daily Bible-reading, which she had been deliberately not doing for the past two weeks, and she read several verses to get caught up to where she knew Seth would be now. One of them was John 14:14, *"You may ask me for anything in my name, and I will do it."* She underlined the words, *'I will do it,'* and she realized God didn't expect her to do anything on her own. Like her mom had said, that's what Jesus was all about: Making us into what we could never be on our own. From God's perspective it was all about her and what He wanted to do in her first—and *then* through her to touch others.

In her journal she wrote this prayer:

> *Make me who you want me to be, Jesus. I give myself to you. My failures, mistakes, all of it. I want to live like you want me to live, resting in your love and grace no matter what.*

She also took out a note card to put on her wall when she got home, and she wrote this phrase on it:

Turning her attention from her heavy thoughts to her stories, she spent most of the remaining hours writing to her heart's content. Now she had two different ones going she thought she might try to tie together, but she wasn't sure how yet. She wrote mostly on the newest one, finishing two more chapters before they arrived home at seven-thirty that evening. She couldn't believe how exhilarating it was, and she wondered if what she had been through emotionally this week somehow made it even sweeter.

Ben was home when they arrived. Spring Break for Western was next week, and she was happy to see him. He hugged her, but she sensed something was wrong.

"What? Why are you looking at me like that?"

"You broke up with Seth?"

She stared at him. "How do you know that?"

"He called me."

"When?"

"Yesterday."

"He's back?"

"He got sick in Mexico. He had a really high fever, so they sent him home. He was in the hospital for two days."

She felt like she couldn't breathe. "Is he okay?"

"Yes. He got home yesterday. He said you wrote him a letter? What's going on, Amber? He's completely devastated by this. He could barely speak to me."

"Ask Mom," she said. "I need to go call him."

She headed upstairs, feeling her whole body trembling. She could barely pick up the phone. When he didn't answer his, she decided to call the house, hoping he hadn't had a relapse and was back in the hospital. A girl answered the phone, and she didn't think it was Kerri. It sounded more like Stephanie.

"Could I speak to Seth, please?"

"I think he's sleeping. Can I have him call you back?"

"Is this Stephanie?"

"Yes."

"Hi, this is Amber."

"Oh, Amber. Hi. Um, he might be awake. I'll go check."

She could tell by the way Stephanie spoke that she knew about the letter. His whole family knew. This was so awful. How could she have ever done such a thing?

It took awhile, but she finally heard his voice. All he said was 'hello', as if he was talking to a stranger.

"Sorry to wake you," she said. "We just got back, and Ben told me you were sick. Are you okay?"

"Yes. Tired but okay. I don't think Mexico is for me."

She didn't know where to begin. "I'm sorry, Seth."

He didn't respond.

"I was going to meet you at the airport on Sunday so we could talk. I never should have sent that letter. I should have told you face to face about how I was feeling."

"Amber, I don't understand. I thought—"

He couldn't finish, and she smiled. He loved her so much. She didn't understand it, but there was no denying it. Seth was rarely at a loss for words.

"It was a lie, Seth," she said gently. "All of it."

"A lie? Our relationship has been a lie?"

"No. The letter. I lied to you, Seth. I didn't mean any of it. I just said all that stuff because I felt like I didn't deserve you, and I didn't see any other way to get you out of my life."

He didn't say anything.

"I'm sorry, Seth. I can't imagine what this week has been like for you, getting sick and ending up in the hospital, and then—" She let the tears fall, feeling awful and hoping he could forgive her. "I'm so sorry. Please forgive me. I need you so much."

"I'm afraid to breathe," he said. "I'm afraid this is a dream, and I'm going to wake up and still not have you."

"It's not a dream. I love you. I promise. Everything is okay."

"Will you come see me tomorrow?"

"Yes. I'll be there, and I'll explain everything. You should rest now. I just had to tell you the truth."

"Say it again."

"What?"

"That you love me, Amber. I need you to love me."

"I love you, Seth. I love you. I love you. I love you."

"I love you too," he said.

"I know you do. I'll see you tomorrow."

"Okay. Bye, sweetheart."

Amber clicked off the phone, feeling sad and elated at the same time. She felt terrible she had put Seth through that, but she was too happy to dwell on it. Her life made sense again. She didn't understand Seth's love for her. She didn't understand God's. But they were here, and she couldn't push them away.

Someone knocked on the door, and she went to open it. Ben had brought her backpack and suitcase up for her, and after setting them on the floor, he asked if everything was all right.

"Yes," she said, accepting the hug he offered her.

"I'm glad, Amber. I wish you could have heard Seth's voice when he called me. I really knew how much he loved you in that moment."

"Thanks Benny. I don't know why I have a hard time believing that."

"I do."

"You do?" she asked, stepping back and waiting for his insight.

"Because you're more focused on the way you see yourself than what God or the rest of us see."

"Do you ever feel that way?"

"All the time, Amber. Hope has been really good for me in that way. When we first started dating, I thought I would be the one encouraging her all the time and having to remind her of God's love, but she knows. She's learned that. And now she's always reminding me. Do you want me to call her? I'm sure she would be more than happy to come over and tell you all about it."

Amber smiled. "I'm sure she would, but I think I get it. I'm going to spend time with Jesus and then get some sleep."

"Are you going to see Seth tomorrow?"

"Yes."

"Hope and I have been writing songs together lately. She writes the words, and I put them to music. There's one I think you might really like. Do you want to hear it?"

"Sure," she said, stepping out of the room and following Ben down the hall to his. He got out his guitar and handed her a copy of the words. It was based on a verse in Colossians that she read first, and then she listened as Ben sang the words to the song.

Yet now he has brought you back as his friends. He has done this through his death on the cross in his own body. As a result he has brought you into the very presence of God, and you are holy and blameless as you stand before him without a single fault.

Colossians 1:22

I will lift up my hands to worship the King
With all that I am, my praise I will bring
Before the throne; By grace I stand
And to You alone, I lift up my hands

I will lift up my voice to sing of Your love
When You poured out Your life, and the mystery of
The mercy that flowed. The blood that You shed,
The passion You showed. . .I will sing of Your love!

There is nothing on earth that can tear me away
From the love that my Savior gave me that day
As I bow before You now
With my soul I will cry out
It's Your love that gives me life
I will sing of Your love

Chapter Eleven

Amber took an early MAX train the following morning and arrived at the downtown station at ten. Kerri was there to pick her up, and they held each other for a long time.

"Is he okay?" she asked, stepping back and wiping her tears.

"He's afraid he's still delirious and won't believe it until he sees you."

"I feel so awful. Is he mad? Truth, Kerri."

"No, Amber. He's not mad. He doesn't quite understand, but he's too relieved to be mad."

"I can explain, really. This is definitely going down as one of my lowest moments."

Kerri laughed and gave her a sideways hug as they walked toward the car. "Well, even you are entitled to some low moments, Amber."

On the way to the house, she did explain to Kerri what she had been feeling, and Kerri understood. "I think we all have moments when we feel that way," she said. "And I remember feeling that way that night too, now that you mention it. I didn't completely agree with some of what Ethan said. He's had a lot of problems in the past, and he's still sorting through some of that. It's great he's more on the right track now, but he tends to see himself as having it all figured out when in reality he still has a long way to go."

"You mean like the rest of us?"

Kerri laughed. "Yes."

"One thing I learned from this is that I need to look at what the Bible has to say, not go by what others say. This isn't the first time I've heard something from other Christians that completely contradicts what the Bible actually says."

"And there have been some things I have read that I thought meant one thing," Kerri added, "but then later God has shown them to me in a different light."

"That exact thing happened to me this morning!"

"Yeah?"

"Jesus says, *'If you love me, you will obey what I command.'* And that's what I was thinking that night and for the last two weeks—If I'm not doing what that person is doing, then I must not love God. But it's not about doing what someone else is doing, it's about doing what He specifically asks *me* to do. And when I'm loving Him, those things come easy to me—so easy it almost seems like nothing."

"Like when He told you *not* to go on the mission trip, and you obeyed?"

"Yes! And now I've seen the reality of why He didn't want me to go: Number one because He wanted Matt to go in my place, and number two because He wanted to show me all of this, and number three because I would have been a complete wreck if I would have been there when Seth got sick and then had to stay behind."

"You mean like he's been since Wednesday?" Kerri said with a smile.

"Is that when he read the letter?"

"Yes, and I was sitting right there," she said as she pulled the car into the driveway. "You brought him to tears in two minutes flat."

Once again she felt awful and wasn't sure she could face him.

"I don't say that to make you feel bad," Kerri added. "I say that because there is someone here who is very anxious to see you."

They both got out of the car, and Kerri led the way to the front door. "What did you think of Lifegate?" she asked.

"I loved it. Mandy did too. We're definitely going."

Kerri smiled. "Me too. You just told me so."

"Me?"

"Well, God did, but through what you said. I've been waiting for some kind of confirmation of exactly where I should go. And when I started seeing Dylan, I thought maybe that was God's way of telling me I'm supposed to go to George Fox with him instead, but I've still been wanting to go to Lifegate, and I think God is trying to show me I'm supposed to, but in a different way. Even though things are going well with Dylan, I still want Lifegate more than I want a relationship right now—and the only explanation for that is because I'm more interested in going where God is leading me than where a great guy wants me to be. I've been thinking, 'But he's so great. How can I let that go?' and God has been saying, 'Trust Me, Kerri. That's where you need to be. You just listen and go, and I'll bring the right guy for you at the right time."

"Does that mean you're breaking up with him?"

"I'm not sure about that yet, but only being friends is probably for the best. That's pretty much been our relationship anyway. He's never kissed me. He wanted to wait until I felt sure about us. And this is telling me I'm not. At least not yet."

Amber smiled. "That's three of us sharing a room. I wonder who the fourth will be."

"Can you keep a secret?"

"From Seth?" she asked, feeling prepared to say she'd rather not know.

"No, he knows. From anyone else, especially Chad."

"Sure. What?"

"I called Jessica about a week ago, just to see how she was doing since I haven't seen her for awhile. She goes to the college group at church, but I hardly ever see her. Anyway, we were talking, and I was telling her about possibly going to Lifegate, and she told me she's been seriously thinking about going to a Christian college next year, but she didn't know where to go, so I told her to check it out, and she called me a few days later and said she wanted to go if I did too."

"Is Chad going there?"

"He hasn't decided yet, and we're not telling him she's probably going. Seth wants to wait and see where God leads him without that factored into it."

"Is Jessica going to camp this summer?"

"Yes. Chad doesn't know that yet either."

Kerri had led her up to Seth's room. "He was sleeping when I left," she said, knocking lightly on the door.

They heard him say to come in, and Kerri opened the door a bit, peeking her head inside and saying, "You ready for a visitor?"

"Get her in here," he said loud enough for Amber to hear.

Kerri stepped back and allowed her to pass by. "I think he's anxious to see you. He's been such a grouch these past couple of days."

Amber laughed. "Sorry. I'll try and cheer him up."

"Yeah, like that's gonna be real tough," Kerri said, stepping away and leaving them alone.

Amber pushed the door open more fully and stepped into the room. Seth was in bed but sitting up against the headboard. He looked pale but otherwise good. After spending the last two weeks thinking she might never see him again, she definitely welcomed the sight of his warm brown eyes and familiar smile.

"Hi," she said, sitting on the edge of the bed and taking his hand. "How are you?"

He pulled her close to him, and she leaned into his chest. He smelled like fresh soap, and she knew he must have just taken a shower. "This has been the longest week of my life, Amber, and there's no other way I would rather have it end."

"I'm sorry—"

"Shh," he said, lifting her chin and kissing her tenderly. "No words right now. I just want to enjoy the fact that you're here."

She remained silent and enjoyed more of his kisses and then leaned against him and listened to the beating of his heart. She wanted to enjoy the fact she was here too, and that he was welcoming her so easily after receiving such a heavy blow. The reality of his love for her hit her afresh.

"I love you, Amber. And I need you. Don't ever doubt that. You're a part of me. Without you I'm not whole."

"I didn't doubt that you loved me, Seth. I thought I needed to convince you that you shouldn't."

She sat up fully and faced him, explaining everything she had been thinking—since the retreat and up until yesterday afternoon when she talked to her mom. He listened without comment until she finished by saying, "I saw on my way here that you tried to call my phone several times, but I didn't take it on the trip. I'm sorry you ended up having to read the letter when you had no way to reach me. That wasn't what I wanted at all. Even though I told you not to call me, deep down I knew you would."

He smiled. "You're right about that."

"I can't believe you called Ben."

"He wasn't much help, so I called Stacey too."

She laughed. "You did? What did she say?"

"She didn't believe me at first, but once I convinced her, she said, 'I'm not buying it, Seth. There's something she's not telling you.' And then she said, 'If Amber is really that stupid, would you mind waiting around for about seven years and then dating my little sister? I'm praying for a guy like you for her. Maybe it's you!'"

Amber laughed and Seth pulled her close to him. She held him in return and allowed his words of grace and truth to sink deep into her heart.

"Just let God love you, and let me love you. That's all you have to do. Failures and mistakes and shortcomings you see in yourself—whether they're real or not, we both love you anyway, just for who you are. We can't stop."

"I know, Seth, and I have to love you both in return because I can't stop. It's not just something I do, it's a part of who I am."

He held her silently for a moment and then asked, "Are we going to Lifegate?"

"Yes! I loved it, Seth. I could totally picture us there together."

"And Mandy?"

"Yes. She loved it too."

"Did Kerri tell you about Jessica?"

"Yep. That's so cool."

"Don't tell Chad."

"I won't."

"How long can you stay?" he asked.

"All day if you want."

"Tomorrow too?"

She smiled. "I suppose I could arrange that."

"I missed you, even before I got the letter."

"I missed you too."

They heard a knock on the open door and they both turned to see Chad standing in the doorway.

"Am I interrupting?" he asked.

"No. Come on in, Chad," Seth said.

"Hi, Amber."

"Hi, Chad," she said, standing up to give him a hug. "How are you?"

"Good. And you?"

"Much better today," she said, wondering if Chad knew about the letter. By what he said next, she supposed he did.

"Yeah, me too. It's good to see you."

Amber decided to ask Chad something, acting as if she hadn't heard anything on the subject from Seth and Kerri. "Are you going back to camp this summer?"

"Yes, I think so," he said. "If they take me back. I sent in my application yesterday."

"You did?" Seth said. "Sweet, man."

Amber continued to play innocent, talking more to Seth than Chad. "Wow, that's a lot of us who are going back this year. You, me, Chad, Kerri, Lexi, Josh, Ben, Hope, Tamara—she's going to be a senior counselor—who else have I heard from?—oh, Lacey, Sara, Jessica, Haley—any guys you know of?"

"Not that I know of," Seth said.

Amber glanced at Chad. "How about you?" she asked. "You got pretty close to Adam and Warner didn't you? Have you heard from them?"

Chad was looking at her, but he didn't appear to have heard the question. "I'm sorry, what?"

She fought to keep a straight face. "Do you know of anyone else who's going back?"

"Uh, no. Not really."

"Well, that's quite a few anyway—plus Matt, Colleen, Stacey, and Kenny. It should be fun."

Chapter Twelve

Seth said he was feeling up to eating something, and the three of them went downstairs. Amber was greeted warmly by his parents, and they seemed to hold on to her a bit longer than usual.

"Good to see you, honey," his mom said. "How was your trip to California?"

"It was nice. I'm glad we went. I can't imagine going to school anywhere else now, unless of course your son changes his mind about where he's going."

Seth pulled her close to him. "Not gonna happen, sweetheart."

His mom spoke again. "I set up the couch for you to lie down, Seth. You three go ahead and relax, and I'll bring you something."

They thanked her and went into the adjoining family room where Seth decided to sit up with her for now. He had been weak all day yesterday and had a lingering headache, but he had more strength today. The three of them talked until Seth's mom brought them sandwiches and fruit, and then Kerri came to join them also.

"Chad's going to camp," Seth said.

"That's great, Chad," Kerri said. "All four of us there again. That should be fun."

He smiled. "I heard there's going to be more than four of us."

"Yes, quite a few." She turned to Seth. "Did you tell him?"

"Yes."

All three of them looked at Chad.

"Now Amber knows too? Why does that not surprise me?"

"It's hard to keep secrets from your girlfriend. You'll find that out."

"No scheming," he warned. "It's gotta be God, not you three."

"We'll be good," Seth answered for them.

When they had finished eating, Amber went upstairs to get something out of her bag she had bought for Seth in California. When she had gotten it, she didn't think she would actually be giving the shirt to him, but when Mandy had suggested it, she didn't have any legitimate reason to say no—It was too perfect for him.

Amber got the t-shirt from her bag and was about to step out of Kerri's bedroom when Stephanie came in. She had her little girl in her arms, who Amber supposed must be getting close to two by now. Alyssa had beautiful blond hair like Stephanie's and big blue eyes also.

"Hi, Stephanie," she said, wondering if she was coming to get something out of Kerri's room.

"Hi, Amber," she said, surprising her with a hug. They had always been friendly with one another, but Amber hadn't spent enough time here to get to know her well. This was the first time Stephanie had hugged her, but she quickly explained. "I'm so glad you weren't serious about breaking up with Seth. He's become like a brother to me, and I've never seen him so broken over anything like he was this week. I was seriously scared he might not have the will to get better."

"He wasn't supposed to come home early," she said, laughing at herself. "Of all the idiotic things I've ever done.

With our history together I should have known it wouldn't go like I planned."

Stephanie smiled at her and set Alyssa down to play with some stuffed animals Kerri had on a chest at the end of her bed. "I know this is probably really bad of me," she said, "but I heard you and Seth talking earlier when you were in his room, and I couldn't resist standing in the hallway and listening to what you had to say."

Amber wasn't surprised they'd been overheard in this house, and she hadn't said anything she wouldn't be comfortable with anyone else hearing, she didn't think. And everything about Stephanie told her she had something specific she wanted to say, or she wouldn't have come in here and told her that. She waited for her to go on.

"Are you mad?" Stephanie asked.

"No," she answered quickly. "Which part did you hear?"

"The part about feeling like you don't deserve him because you don't love God enough. I know that's not true. Seth is always talking about how great you are, and I've often wished I could be more like you and find a great guy like Seth. But it's sort of nice for me to know you sometimes feel like I do a lot of the time."

"How do you feel?"

"Like I mess up everything. Like I'm never going to be like you or Kerri. Like I'm only nineteen and I already screwed up my life so bad, there's no hope for me."

"That's not true, Steph."

"I know. And I'm working on believing that, but I wanted to tell you seeing someone like you almost walk away from Seth makes me realize that some days we make good choices and other days not so good, but it can all work out in the end."

"I'm learning that too," she said. "And no matter how on-top-of-it others see me, or I see myself, it all comes down to leaving myself and every day in God's hands. That's what I lost sight of—His grace. I thought it was all about what I should be doing, instead of what He's already done for me and will keep doing as long as I trust Him with my imperfect self."

"Seth thinks you're perfect."

She laughed. "Well, I'm not. I promise. Perfect for him, maybe, but I have plenty of flaws, believe me."

"Like trying to dump the most perfect boyfriend on the planet?"

"Yes, don't try that," she laughed. "It doesn't work!"

Stephanie appeared thoughtful, and Amber added something else.

"Did you hear the part about what my mom said to me?"

"About not being able to stop others from loving you?"

"Yes. I get caught up in that a lot, thinking I have somehow earned God's love or the love of others, instead of it being something they can't help but do."

"Me too," she said. "That's pretty much how I ended up pregnant at sixteen. I was trying to earn a guy's love, so I gave him what he wanted, but that just got me pregnant, not love."

Stephanie was quiet for a moment and then continued. "But the really sad part is, I'm shutting out some love that is there, that I could have without condition."

"From who?"

"My mom. She freaked out when I told her I was pregnant, and she wanted me to have an abortion. In some ways I kept Alyssa to rebel against her. That's how I ended up living here, which I know is where I needed to be, but my mom has contacted me several times, apologized to me for driving us away, and she's invited me to come home, but I've been putting her off."

"You're her daughter, Steph. She can't stop loving you any more than you could stop loving Alyssa."

"I've told myself I don't want to go home because it won't be like it is here, and I'm sure it won't, but that's part of trusting God, isn't it? Trusting Him to work through imperfect situations and imperfect people?"

"That's how you ended up here."

"Yes," she said. "If I move back home, could I write to you sometimes? Having someone like you to talk to could really help, I think. I know you'll be off to camp soon and then to college, so if you can't write back—"

"I'll write you," she said.

"You will?"

"Yes."

"Why?"

"Because I love writing letters, and I love talking about what God is doing in my life and hearing what others have to say. That's one of the reasons I fell for Seth. I'd never met anyone who liked to write letters more than me."

Alyssa had walked over to Kerri's desk and was starting to get into things, so Stephanie went to pull her away. That was when Amber saw it: The grace of God working in yet another way. God had taken a mistake that Stephanie had made—a huge, life-changing mistake, and He'd made something wonderful out of it. A beautiful little girl; A restored young woman who now knew Him as the Lover of her soul; And perhaps a restored relationship between Stephanie and her mom that would be stronger than ever if Stephanie allowed God to take her home and make things right.

She knew if God could do that for Stephanie, He could do the same for her no matter what she faced in the future. Mistakes she made, bad decisions, difficult circumstances, others hurting her in some way—God could take it all and make something beautiful out of her life if she continued to trust Him and hide herself in His perfect love.

Later that afternoon, Seth felt tired and fell asleep on the couch. Chad had left to go to work, and Kerri was upstairs working on a project for one of her classes. Amber took out her laptop and settled herself in the big overstuffed chair in the corner of the family room. She was still writing, working on the fourth chapter of the book she had started on Thursday, when Seth woke up.

She went to see if he needed anything, and he said he could use some water, so she went to refill his glass. When she returned, he sat up and took a drink and then asked her what she was working on.

"A story," she said.

"The one about Stacey?"

She hesitated to tell him but went ahead. "No, this is another one I started on the trip."

"What's it about?"

"I can't tell you."

"Why not?"

"I just can't, okay?"

"Okay," he said.

She was glad he let it go, but she felt bad about lying to him when he had asked her directly if Mandy liked Matt. It would be one thing for her to never mention it to him, but to outright lie was another, and she didn't feel right about it. There was also a part of her that wondered why Seth had asked. Had Matt said something to him about Mandy, and he was trying to find out for his friend if the feeling was mutual? If so, she could be cheating her cousin out of something with Matt without even knowing it. Maybe Matt had asked Seth not to say anything to her either unless Mandy felt the same way.

She had promised Mandy she wouldn't tell him, so she felt torn. But then she had another thought. Yes, she had lied to Seth, and that was wrong. She should have said, 'I can't answer that,' which would have given it away anyway, but she wouldn't have been telling him directly like Mandy had asked her not to. So, she decided to do the next best thing.

"Do you remember asking me something in the van just before we left the retreat center two weeks ago?"

"I asked if you were all right, and you told me you were."

"Yeah, I lied."

"I sort of figured that out," he said.

"I lied to you about another thing too. Do you remember asking me anything else?"

He thought for a moment. "About Mandy?"

She nodded. "Don't ask me again, because I can't tell you, but I'm confessing my dishonesty to you because I don't want any secrets between us, okay?"

He smiled. "Okay. I don't know that she likes him, and you don't know he likes her, because I'm not supposed to tell you either."

She started to say something, but he stopped her with his fingers on her lips. "We'll let them figure it out, okay? If it's meant to be, Jesus will help them find each other. Four years at Lifegate should be plenty of time for Him to work with."

She knew he was right, and she smiled. She was at that same place in her story, and she had been trying to decide if someone would spill the beans about them liking each other, or if they would have to discover it some other way, and she knew what would be better.

"Okay," she said, giving him a sweet kiss. Knowing Matt liked Mandy put her in an incredibly romantic mood.

"I love you, Seth. I'm glad Jesus helped us find each other, even if it's complicated sometimes."

He smiled. "Me too, Amber. And thinking I'd lost you makes me love you even more, but don't you dare ever do that to me again."

"I won't. I promise."

He leaned to kiss her, but Amber saw someone enter the room, and she shifted her eyes to see Seth's brother had arrived as they had been expecting sometime today. Seth followed her gaze and saw Micah as well.

"Hey, Mike. You made it."

"I did," he said, coming over to stand beside the couch. "You look awful."

"You should have seen me three days ago."

Stephanie came into the room, and Micah turned to look at her. A pleasant smile formed on his face, and he stepped over to give her a hug.

"Hey, Steph," he said. "You look great. Where's Lyssa?"

"Napping," she said. "How are you? I haven't seen you in forever."

"I know. It's been a busy term."

The four of them ended up staying in the room and talking for quite some time. Seth's mom had gone to the pregnancy center this afternoon, and Seth's dad was around but had disappeared somewhere. When he finally appeared and realized Micah was here, he said he hadn't heard him come in and wondered how long ago he had arrived.

"About an hour," Micah replied.

A few minutes later, one of the other girls who lived with Seth's family came downstairs with Alyssa in her arms. "I heard her crying and thought I'd bring her down," Kim said to Stephanie as she handed her over.

"Thanks," Stephanie said, taking the sleepy-eyed girl into her arms. Alyssa laid her head on her shoulder but was turned so Micah could see her little face.

He smiled and reached out to stroke Alyssa's bare arm. "Hi, sweetie. Look how big you are."

Alyssa didn't turn away or appear threatened by Micah's presence. He said a few more things to her and then Stephanie asked if she was hungry.

"I should probably get her something," she said, starting to rise from the small sofa where she and Micah had been sitting together for the past hour.

"Here, I'll take her," Micah said, holding out his hands and accepting a calm Alyssa into his arms while Stephanie stepped away into the adjacent kitchen to get her daughter a snack.

Amber had a thought that was strengthened as the evening progressed. She had once asked Seth if he or his brothers had ever seen the girls they took into their home as anything besides temporary sisters, which is how Seth had said he viewed them. Seth said he never had, but he didn't know about Micah and Zachary. He knew they had never actually dated any of them, but he supposed they may have been attracted to some at one point or another.

Amber had seen Micah and Stephanie together before. Stephanie had been living here for two years, and Amber had often viewed her as being Seth's sister. That's the way he treated her—like a part of the family, and Micah always had too. But watching them together during dinner and into the evening, Amber was almost certain there was something different about the way Micah looked at Stephanie and the way Stephanie looked at him. It was almost like something had started the last time Micah had been home for an extended time during Winter Break, and now they were picking up where they'd left off and wondering if the other person had missed them too.

Chapter Thirteen

"Amber! I can't believe you!"

Amber stopped writing mid-word and looked up from her journal at Kerri. With Seth feeling tired this evening, he had gone to bed early and she was sitting up in Kerri's bed, having a second time with Jesus after this emotional day.

"What?" she asked, having no idea what Kerri was talking about. What had she done now?

"What!" Kerri laughed. "Do you know how long I've been trying to get Stephanie to go back home, how many times I've talked to her and gotten nowhere? And then you come here, talk to her for ten minutes, and she decides to go!"

Amber shook her head. "She decided all on her own. All I did was listen. I didn't even know she had that option until she told me."

Kerri didn't appear convinced.

"How long has she been putting it off?"

"For a year."

"A year? Wow. I didn't know it had been that long."

"See what I mean!"

Amber laughed. "She's going? She told you that?"

"She told my mom and dad tonight after dinner, and when they asked what made her decide, she said, 'It was something Amber said. She made me realize I'm trying to keep my mom from loving me, but I can't. She'll love me no matter what, but this way I'm missing it.'"

Amber smiled. That had been something she had said when she was talking to Seth, not to Stephanie directly, but she didn't tell her Stephanie had been listening in the hallway. However it had happened, she was glad it had.

"See! I can't believe you!" Kerri said in mock anger. "I'm never speaking to you again."

Amber laughed. "It wasn't me," she repeated. "It was totally God. I am not taking credit for that."

Amber supposed Seth didn't know about Stephanie's decision yet, but by the time she had showered and dressed the following morning and met him downstairs to do their daily reading together, he had heard all about it and had similar words for her.

"It wasn't me!" she insisted. "Jesus was all over that. She just happened to be listening."

"But you said the right thing."

Amber lowered her voice so she wouldn't be overheard. "But I was talking to you about me, not to Steph."

"What?"

"She overheard us talking after I got here yesterday. All that stuff I said about letting God and others love me, not because I deserve it but because they will whether I choose accept it or not—that's what she heard, and that's what made the difference."

"You never talked to her directly?"

"Well, yes. Later. But she came to me, and all I did was listen and restate what I'd already said."

Seth smiled at her. "You don't see it, do you?"

"See what?"

He paused, seeming to collect his thoughts and then explained. "You know, when you were telling me all that yesterday, one thing I was thinking, but I didn't say, is that you could do a lot more in terms of mentoring other girls in your youth group or talking to others about God at school if you had a little more confidence in yourself and God's ability to use you."

Amber instantly began to have similar feelings she had been battling for the past two weeks. She didn't know how to get that confidence, and she began to feel defeated once again, but Seth kept talking.

"But then later on, I was considering talking to you about it, and I clearly heard God saying, 'No, Seth. That's not right.' I didn't understand why, but I kept my thoughts to myself anyway, and I'm glad I did because I just now realized something—something that's been right in front of me ever since I've known you, but I've never seen it before."

"What?"

"Most of us try to force ministry. We try to decide what we're going to do for God, and then do it, but you don't do that. You wait for God to bring it to you. And that's why everything you touch turns to gold."

Amber didn't respond, sort of seeing what Seth was saying. She'd never thought about it before either.

"And when I look at myself, I see the same thing. When I got sick in Mexico again, I was like, 'God, this isn't supposed to happen. Why did you bring me here if I was going to be more of a hassle than a help?' And I heard God saying, 'I will use you however I please, Seth. More is going on here than you can see. You don't decide how you're going to serve Me, I have plans for you, not the other way around.'

"And then after I talked to you, I could see a little bit of what God was doing. Me going to Mexico, you writing that letter, and me coming home early was all a part of a way He was working in our lives—yours and mine—to teach us something about ourselves, our relationship, and our relationship with Him."

"And you going was about getting Matt to go?"

"Yes, exactly," he said. "And that wasn't my plan. My plan was for you and me to go and have this great ministry experience together, but God's plan was to get Matt there and take you and me deeper with Him. It's not about what we can do for Him, it's about what He can do for us!"

Amber began to think about all the ways God had used her in the lives of her family members and friends, and girls she'd met at camp, and she could see how most of it wasn't anything she had planned but that God had brought her way.

"We just need to stay close to Him, sweetheart. Stay close, and listen, and live the way He says is right, and He'll take care of the rest."

She smiled. "Isn't that what I said yesterday?"

"Yes. And I thought I knew that already, but I didn't. Not really. I know it, but I don't always live like it. When you see me trying to work stuff out in my own way and make things happen, which I know I do all the time, remind me I don't have to."

They spent time looking up some verses to confirm what they were learning about God's grace and how He worked in their lives, and many of them were verses she knew well but hadn't seen the truth of in that way. Her favorite was John 15:4, words spoken by Jesus: *"Remain in me, and I will remain in you. No branch can bear fruit by itself; it must remain in the vine. Neither can you bear fruit unless you remain in me."*

They each wrote their personal thoughts, and Amber wrote out a prayer also, thanking God for all He had done in her life and heart this week: for reminding her who she was and what she needed to continue to do—seek Him with all of her heart and leave the rest up to Him; She also thanked Him for working through her to touch others like Stephanie. And then she wrote out this short poem:

In His love I will dwell
In His peace I will rest
In His grace I will stand

***

Seth wanted to go to the airport and welcome Matt and the others from the mission team as they arrived. Everyone was very happy to see Seth alive and well. There had been no way to contact them until late last night, and the last they'd heard, Seth had a fever of 105 and they had no idea what was wrong, reminding Amber once again she was meant to be here, not where she would've had to wait to find out if he was all right.

Matt held on to him for a long time, and it was obvious how much Matt appreciated Seth and his friendship. He didn't say much except, "Man, don't scare us like that."

"How did the rest of the week go?" Seth asked.

"Good," Matt said. "Having you leave really brought the rest of us together, and God did some great stuff. We got a lot of good video for you to cut up and put together."

"Sounds like fun," Seth said.

They said good-bye to Matt and the others there and then Seth drove her home and stayed into the evening. He was feeling better but somewhat weak and tired, so she insisted he leave at a decent hour so he wouldn't be driving too late. He gave her several sweet kisses outside the door and told her he would call when he got home to let her know he had made it safely.

"I know God would carry me if I ever lost you, Seth, but I really hope that doesn't happen. I love loving you."

"I love loving you, Amber. I can't stop, so don't try and make me."

"Okay. I won't."

She ended up having a really great week. Softball practice started, and the weather was nice enough for them to be outside, and she could see they had the makings of a great team this year. She had a fun time with her teammates every afternoon too. In the past she'd had those she liked and got along well with and others she tolerated, like Paige and another girl named Robyn who was very bossy. She was their best player, and she knew it.

But this season Amber found herself seeing others differently. She was happy to be playing a sport she loved, and even if girls like Paige and Robyn tended to be arrogant and thought they could tell everyone what to do, she realized they were good players and she could have more fun because of their skills. It was more fun to win than lose, and with Paige at second base and Robyn at first and both of them being killer hitters, they were key players who often made her job as pitcher easier. The more outs they got, the less pitches she had to throw.

She also had a feeling God was going to use her in the lives of her teammates. It had been her connection with Stacey in softball two years ago that had led to Stacey going to camp with her that summer. She didn't have any specific plans to invite anyone to church or start a Bible study or have a weekend slumber party, but she felt ready for whatever God wanted to do through her—whenever, wherever, however He pleased.

She kept thinking about John 14:14: *"You may ask me for anything in my name and I will do it."* But she wasn't sure what to ask for. Seeing her whole team come to know Jesus would certainly be exciting and something she believed He could do, but was that a part of His plan, or just her own idea? She didn't want to be demanding anything. She had done that in the past and ended up frustrated and confused when she didn't see anything happen.

On Friday morning before she left for school, she saw the words a bit differently. *"You may ask me for anything in my name, and I will do it."*—Not, 'I will help *you* do it', or 'I will do it *through* you', or 'I will do it *your way'*, or even 'You will *see* Me do it', just *'I will'*. And she realized all she needed to do was ask. That's it. That was her only guaranteed role.

God may choose to use her, but He might have a better way, or He might do something through her she would never be aware of—but none of that was her concern. He only wanted her to ask.

> *Jesus, I believe you can do anything. I believe I can ask you for anything, and you will hear me, and you will do things I see as impossible. You have given me a love for my softball teammates who do not know you, but I don't know how to reach them. I trust that you do and you love them enough to do so. I ask that you would reveal yourself to them, through me or some other way, this softball season or sometime in the future—whenever they are most ready to meet you. May they know you like I have come to know you. Give them eyes to see, ears to hear, and hearts to believe in you.*

Chapter Fourteen

Amber headed downstairs, had a bowl of cereal, and was about to head out the door, knowing Stacey would be here any minute, when her mom asked her something.

"I was thinking of calling Aunt Beth today and seeing if she wanted to have lunch and then go shopping for the afternoon. Is there anything you need I could pick up for you?"

"I don't really need anything right now, but if you see something cute to wear, feel free to buy it for me."

Her mom laughed. "Okay, I'll keep that in mind."

"How is Aunt Beth?"

"I think she's okay. It was a difficult step to move here, but she knows it was the right one."

She heard Stacey's car pulling up and grabbed her backpack from the chair. "Have fun," she said. "I should be home normal time."

"Okay. Bye, sweetie. Have a good day."

She went out and joined Stacey in the car on another sunny spring morning. March was often a wet month, so this week had been a nice change and made her feel like summer wasn't too far off.

On the way to school, she thought about Mandy, wondering if she should do what she had been thinking about since last night. One of the things she had been doing this week during her prayer time was asking God to show her what He specifically wanted her to do. And the only thing she kept hearing God say was, 'Talk to Mandy.'

She was happy to do that except for one thing. She didn't know what exactly she was supposed to talk to her about. Several possibilities came to mind. Since the retreat, Mandy had seemed down, and she didn't know if that was because of Matt or something else. She also thought Mandy might be mad at her. With her busy schedule, it had been difficult to find time to spend with her, and Mandy may have been expecting a lot more when she moved here. Mandy had gotten to know her other friends, and they were all nice to her, but she hadn't become close friends with them, and Amber didn't think Mandy had connected with anyone else on her own either.

Since she had softball practice after school, she decided to talk to her at lunch and be blunt, letting her know God was laying her on her heart to ask if anything was wrong. At first Mandy said no, but Amber waited for a moment, allowing the silence to linger between them, and then Mandy was more honest.

"Well, yes," she said.

"What?"

Mandy looked like she might cry.

"Mandy, just tell me," she said gently.

"I can't."

"Why not?"

She didn't respond.

"Are you mad at me?"

"No."

"Does this have anything to do with me?"

Silence.

"It does?"

Mandy glanced at her but then looked away.

"Okay, what did I do?"

"Nothing."

"Mandy! It's not nothing. Tell me."

"You didn't do anything, Amber. I'm just jealous of you, and I don't know how to stop feeling this way."

"Jealous of me? About what?"

"The person you are. You're pretty and fun and talented, and so solid with Jesus, and you've got a great boyfriend and other friends who love you—including me—and wish I was more like you instead of, well, me."

"Except for the boyfriend thing, you have all of that too."

Mandy rolled her eyes.

"Mandy! You're pretty and fun and way smarter than me. I know you haven't formed any close friendships here except with me, but everyone loves you. These are friends I've had for years because I've been here for years, not two months."

"Amber, just forget it. I shouldn't have said anything. I know you don't understand, and that's okay. You don't have to."

"Understand what?"

"Me. The way I am and how much I hate it."

"What do you hate?"

"I'm shy and quiet and never know what to say. I dream about a guy like Matt, but I would never know what to say to him, if by some miracle he actually asked me out."

"Is that why you're not going to camp with me this summer?"

"Sort of. Not because of Matt, but because I won't know anyone there except you, and I can imagine it being like this."

"Like what?"

"You being my friend but everyone else's at the same time. I don't expect you to not be that way, I just wish I was like that. It's me, Amber. Not you."

Amber thought before she spoke. She didn't understand why Mandy saw herself the way she did. In Amber's opinion that was her only flaw. She was incredibly sweet. She never said anything bad about anyone. She was very smart. Beautiful. The type of person anyone would want for a friend, but at the same time she put up this wall around herself that kept others from going beneath the surface. She had dropped it with her, and Colleen somewhat. But even being around Stacey or Nicole or Seth seemed to make her put it back up again.

She thought about the things Seth and Kerri had said about Dylan, and she knew Mandy was like he used to be. She hadn't talked to Mandy about him, and Mandy only knew him from the retreat.

"Do you remember Dylan?"

"Kerri's boyfriend?"

"Yes. Would it surprise you to know he used to be very shy and quiet too?"

"Amber, I don't need a lecture about coming out of my shell and suddenly being Miss Personality. I'm not that way, and I never will be."

Amber had been about to suggest that Mandy come with her to camp this year—to get out of her comfort zone, but maybe that wasn't the right solution. She didn't want to be telling her what to do with her summer, that was up to Mandy to decide. Instead she said something she hadn't planned to say but was based on what she had learned over the last few weeks about herself.

"Maybe instead of hating yourself for the way you are, you should accept it and embrace it."

"What do you mean?"

"I mean, what's wrong with being quiet and shy? Personally, I like quiet people more than those who are always running off at the mouth, talking about stuff I couldn't care less about. Being quiet can be a beautiful thing, Mandy. It's one of the things I like about you. You need to see it that way instead of thinking you need to be like me."

Mandy didn't reply, but she seemed to be less resistant to this than what she had said so far.

"You know one of the things I discovered about Seth after I'd been dating him for awhile?"

"What?"

"He's actually a quiet person. He wasn't like that with me in the beginning because he had to talk to get me to talk. But when we go someplace where he doesn't know a lot of people or he's around those who do talk a lot, he's more quiet. I really saw that when we were at camp together last summer. Sure he does things like act on stage in front of a bunch of people, but that's different for him than just hanging out. He talks when he has something to say, but he often chooses to be quiet and listen instead."

"And you like that about him?"

"Yes. I think it's one of his greatest qualities."

Amber wanted to tell her so badly that Matt liked her, but she kept it to herself. She had an idea she wanted to run by Seth before she mentioned anything to Mandy about it. And maybe Mandy needed to become comfortable with herself rather than finding her worth in the eyes of someone else. As Seth had said, four years at Lifegate was a long time. She just hoped Mandy didn't change her mind about going.

For now she gave Mandy a hug and said, "You don't have to be anyone besides you. I like you the way you are, and I know I'm not the only one. Work on believing that, okay?"

"Okay," she said.

The following afternoon when Amber saw Seth, she asked him if he would think about talking to Matt and see if Matt would like to ask Mandy to the prom so the four of them could go together.

"Sure, I'll ask him," he said.

"That's not meddling too much, is it?"

He smiled. "Actually I was already thinking of suggesting that to him."

"I should have known," she said, giving him a light kiss. "You're as hopeless as me, Mr. Romance."

"Speaking of romance," he said. "How about if we go to the lake and take a canoe ride today?"

"Sounds perfect."

They went to find her dad and asked if he could follow them to the lake and bring the canoe in his truck. He said he would help them tie it down but Seth could drive the truck himself.

"You'll let me drive your truck?" Seth asked.

"Sure. If I can trust you to take my daughter to California, I can certainly trust you to drive my truck ten miles."

After they were headed for the lake, Seth asked her something based on her dad's comment.

"Do you trust me to take care of you in California?"

"Yes. You always take care of me."

"But Lifegate will be a whole new world for us."

"Yes, I suppose it will, but you'll still be you, and I'll still be me, and we'll have good accountability around us. Kerri won't let you get away with anything."

"Yeah, I know," he said.

"Has she told Dylan she's going?"

"Yes."

"How did he take it?"

"He asked her to consider keeping things as they are—continuing to see him until the summer, and then once they're separated, having an understanding they are both free to see other people, but to write to each other and remain close friends with the possibility of something more."

"Is she considering it?"

"Yes, but I have the feeling she's going to tell him she doesn't want to—mainly because she doesn't think she's the right girl for him and she would hate to see him hang on to her instead of taking a risk with someone else."

Amber was hesitant to say anything to Seth about what she had witnessed between Micah and Stephanie last weekend. She had been so wrong about Kerri liking Chad last fall, but she had been thinking about them off and on.

"Did you have a lot of time with Micah this week?" she asked.

"Yes. For once we were both not busy."

"He seemed different to me this time," she said. "Does he have a girlfriend?"

"Not that I know of," Seth said. "But he did seem happier, now that you mention it."

She decided to say it. "I think he likes Stephanie."

"What makes you say that?"

"I've seen them together before, but they seemed different this time. But maybe it was just me, or maybe they've both changed a lot."

Seth seemed deep in thought for a moment, and a smile slowly emerged. "I think you may have something there," he finally said. "I didn't think about it. Steph's like a part of the family to me now, but I don't remember Mike talking to her as much before. And when he found out she was moving back home, he seemed happy for her but said something about her having to come visit a lot, which isn't like him."

"Do you think that would be a good thing—them getting together?"

"Sure," he said. "Steph could definitely use a guy like Mike, and she would be good for him."

"How so?"

"Mike's pretty serious most of the time. She would show him a fun and more spontaneous side of life."

When they got to the lake, they enjoyed a long, relaxing canoe ride. The air was a little cold, even with the blue skies overhead, so she was glad she had worn her warmest hoodie. She told him about her prayer for her softball teammates and about talking to Mandy yesterday. He told her about the great stuff that had happened on the mission trip and how much Matt had been impacted through his time there. He had been doing well the last few months, but the trip had changed him in ways Seth had never considered. Seth getting sick had taught Matt a lot about prayer, and the ministry he had been involved in had reminded Matt of how much he had to be thankful for and what a difference knowing God made in his life.

"I'm getting to the point where I'm really longing for camp," she said. "Last year I was excited about going, sort of like I'm excited now about going to college, but I feel different about camp this time—like I don't just want to be there, but I *need* to be there."

"I know what you mean," he said. "That's where it all began. You and me. Both of us going deeper with Jesus."

Thinking back to that first canoe ride with Seth, she knew she had felt hopeful but had no idea what was to come. And the thing that stood out most in her mind were moments like this where they were being themselves and enjoying being together. It didn't matter what they did or where they were, their hearts always seemed to connect. Today marked an anniversary of their first official date. He had asked her to be his girlfriend one year and seven months ago today.

"Do you remember that first canoe ride we took here?" she asked him.

"Yes."

"Do you remember the question I asked you?"

"About if I would mind if you were the only girlfriend I ever had?"

"Yes." She smiled. "I can't believe I asked you that."

"It was a good question, Amber," he said, taking her hands in his. "It made me realize how much I was enjoying our time together because I didn't feel threatened at all by the possibility. In fact, I knew I wanted that very much, but I wasn't sure I could convince you to be mine forever."

"What? Why not?"

"Because you didn't know me that well and I thought you might discover something you didn't like."

She smiled. "Didn't happen, sweet thing. And here we are a year and a half later."

"I'm glad, sweetheart. You're the one I want. My world completely stopped when I got that letter from you. I'm sure I would have gone on somehow, but it would have taken me a very long time to get you out of my heart."

"Have you forgiven me, Seth? You don't have to pretend you're fine if you're not."

"As long as I know you love me, Amber, I'm fine—but are you sure there wasn't anything honest in what you said—like wishing we would have met a few years from now when you knew more about who you were without me invading your identity?"

She smiled. "That was a pretty convincing letter, wasn't it?"

He didn't appear amused.

She laughed. "You're dating a writer now, sweet thing. Watch out."

He smiled, but she knew he wanted an answer, and she didn't have to think twice about her response.

"You're a part of me, Seth. You are a part of who I am becoming. And God knew the perfect time for me to meet you. You have changed my life, but unlike what I said in the letter, I consider that to be a good thing—a vital part of God's plan for me."

Seth leaned forward. Amber closed her eyes, and Seth kissed her. Amber could feel things had changed between them. She had been in love with him before and knew the feeling was mutual, but a deeper form of love had taken over their hearts. Love for each other. Love for God. And a deeper belief in His love for them.

"Where do we go from here?" she asked.

"In the same direction we've been heading all along."

"And where is that?"

He smiled. "To a place called forever."

"Sounds like a good place," she said.

"Does it?"

"Yes."

"Do you want to marry me someday, Amber?"

"Yes."

"Why?"

"Because I love you and I can't handle being away from you for very long; and because I know you want to marry me, and I could never shut out that love. I want it, and I need it. Loving you is like breathing to me, Seth. I don't have to think about it. It just happens."

"I feel the same way, Amber. Let's not stop, okay?"

"Okay." She smiled and received another sweet kiss from the person who knew her better than anyone. From her best friend, now and always.

I'd love to hear how God has used this story to touch your heart.

Write me at:

living_loved@yahoo.com

Made in the USA
Monee, IL
06 December 2020

50958264R00079